YOUR CONSTANT STAR

YOUR CONSTANT STAR

BRENDA HASIUK

ORCA BOOK PUBLISHERS

Library and Archives Canada Cataloguing in Publication

Hasiuk, Brenda, 1968-, author
Your constant star / Brenda Hasiuk.

Issued in print and electronic formats.
ISBN 978-1-4598-0368-8 (pbk.).--
ISBN 978-1-4598-0369-5 (pdf).--ISBN 978-1-4598-0370-1 (epub)

I. Title.
PS8615.A776Y69 2014   jC813'.6   C2013-906653-5
C2013-906654-3

First published in the United States, 2014
Library of Congress Control Number: 2013954147

Summary: Three Winnipeg teens deal with pregnancy,
cultural differences and the fallout of bad decisions.

*Orca Book Publishers is dedicated to preserving the environment and
has printed this book on Forest Stewardship Council® certified paper.*

Orca Book Publishers gratefully acknowledges the support for its publishing programs
provided by the following agencies: the Government of Canada through the Canada Book
Fund and the Canada Council for the Arts, and the Province of British Columbia
through the BC Arts Council and the Book Publishing Tax Credit.

MANITOBA ARTS COUNCIL
CONSEIL DES ARTS DU MANITOBA
With the generous support of the Manitoba Arts Council

Cover design by Chantal Gabriell
Cover images by Getty Images, Dreamstime and iStockphoto.com
Author photo by Ian McCausland

ORCA BOOK PUBLISHERS   ORCA BOOK PUBLISHERS
PO Box 5626, Stn. B   PO Box 468
Victoria, BC Canada   Custer, WA USA
V8R 6S4   98240-0468

www.orcabook.com
Printed and bound in Canada.

17 16 15 14 • 4 3 2 1

To Duncan, my North Star,
and to Sebastian and Katya, our Big and Little Dippers

PART ONE

Faye

ONE

Up until now, I've been pretty much happy ho-hum—and I'm good with that. The only thing remotely interesting about me is that my parents are white and I'm Chinese.

I never thought I'd become obsessed with a Belarusian with bad teeth who called me "little bird." In hindsight, it seems such a strange and condescending thing to call someone whose pants you're trying to get into. But at the time, it turned me weak as a newborn chick. I've spent the last few months hoping some guy who lives almost halfway around the world will get in touch, send me a line like *hey, how you doing*, or *I think about you, little bird, each hour of the day and each of the night*. And I definitely never thought I'd hear from Bev Novak again.

But here I am, on my way to meet a girl I haven't seen since I was eight, almost a decade ago. She moved away, but it probably took her about a minute to track me down. I still live in the same house, on the same street. Happy ho-hum.

It's March in Winnipeg, which means it's snowing— not floating, intricate, wondrous flakes, but pellets that bounce off your face like Ping-Pong balls. Everything is monochromatic—white sky, white ground, white stucco strip mall. My father likes to point out that we live in the coldest major city in the world, as if that's some kind of tourist draw. I told him that calling this week off from school "spring break" is like calling a dentist chair a poolside lounger, and he told me, seriously, that I might have a future in comedy writing.

I don't even know why I agreed to meet up with Bev, because when I think of her, there are no warm and fuzzy childhood vibes. She only lived across the street for three years, and for one of those years, I barely saw her, thanks to what my mother calls "the scissors incident."

I didn't bother mentioning to my parents that I was going to see her again. I knew it'd end up being more trouble than it was worth. Bev and I were both five when we met, and even then, I knew there was nothing ho-hum about Bev.

I'd suggested we meet at the big coffee chain on the corner, the one my father shuns for its "overpriced mediocrity." She's already standing in the doorway, unmistakable, and any thoughts I had of bolting shrivel up. She's talking on her cell and holds up a finger to me.

I can't tell if I'm supposed to wait for her or go in and order. My father likes to joke that the Chinese obsession with duty and etiquette must be genetic, because I get hung up on these things, as if there has to be a right answer for everything. It wasn't quite so funny when I was diagnosed as "borderline OCD," but he's right. They've managed to raise the girl everyone thinks of when they think of Asian girls—I play the cello (or at least I used to), I'm near the top of the class, I sweat the small stuff, I am small-boned and flat-chested.

Bev keeps talking, and it looks like things are getting a little heated, so I go inside. There's no one in the place except a serious-looking guy on a laptop and two older women poring over a photo album. The two girls behind the counter have matching dyed black hair and black T-shirts. One is busy arranging cookies on a tray while the other sits on a stool, watching her.

I stare up at the menu as if I've never seen it before.

"Forget it, just forget it—I'm not your little puppy."

It's Bev. Right behind me. Shouting.

The guy on the laptop looks up, annoyed by the interruption but unable to help himself, like someone just switched his channel from the weather report to reality TV.

"I don't have to listen to this," Bev says and hangs up.

The busy girl waves her hand in front of my face. "Can I get you something?"

Bev spins me around by the shoulders and looks me up and down with a giant smile. Back when I knew her, her two front teeth were crooked, but now they're perfect. "You look the same, Faye," she says. "The very same."

When we were kids, I remember, even when something was a matter of opinion, her enthusiasm always made it *sound* true.

"That's me," I say, trying to ignore Mr. Laptop's gaze, pretending I don't care that the girls behind the counter will bitch about us later. "The very same."

Bev shoves the cell in her purse, which is either very expensive or a *great* knockoff. She unzips her parka and rests her hands on her bulging stomach. There's maybe a two-inch gap of unbelievably tight pink skin between the waist of her yoga pants and the hem of her T-shirt. "I guess you can't say the same thing about me."

Some things are still the same, I want to say. When we were kids, Jill, Bev's half-sister in Toronto, was forever sending her high-priced designer hand-me-downs that didn't suit Bev's baby fat.

It's amazing how much she looks like her mother, Lara, now—nothing but gorgeous, soft curves from head to toe, light eyes darkened by flaky mascara and something else much less obvious. Like a peach that's gotten too ripe.

"You look like your mom," I say.

Bev stares up at the menu as if bored by the very mention of her mother. "Yeah, you should see her now. She put on, like, a gazillion pounds, then she lost it, and now she's back up to a size eighteen."

The busy girl gives up on us and starts refilling a stack of cup lids. The other one still does nothing except raise her eyebrows at me. One of them is pierced and looks slightly infected.

"She's teaching classes on emotional eating," Bev says. "Which is too funny for words."

I fish out the gift card my old cello teacher gave me for Chinese New Year and tell Bev I'm buying—whatever she wants. When our drinks are ready, I manage to get her to take a seat by the faux fireplace. She sinks down onto a purple faux-suede armchair and flashes her now-perfect teeth. She doesn't say a word, just smiles with one pink hand resting peacefully on her pink bump.

"So," I say. "Wow." Then what? What does one say in these circumstances? *So, you decided not to abort?*

She blows on her super-grande mocha, then takes a long, beer-like chug. Foam lingers on her upper lip, and she wipes it off with the back of her hand. For the first time, she seems to notice Mr. Laptop's gaze, and she glares at him until he goes back to staring at his screen.

"Obviously, this was not planned," she says.

I nod, thankful I have a tea bag to play with.

She plants her coffee on the wobbly table and pushes it away like it suddenly smells bad. "My dad is royally pissed, but that's nothing new." She pats her stomach. "The baby daddy, Mannie, isn't very bright and is very into the whole thing."

I nod some more, like I have a clue. I can barely remember what Bev's father looked like, maybe because he was almost never there. You just always felt his presence, after the fact. Bev would say, "He filled in the pool because Mom is too lazy to do a damn thing around here," or "He went to New Orleans and didn't take us, so she's ripping out the carpet and putting in hardwood."

"What about your mom?" I ask.

Bev laughs with the raspiness of a smoker. I remember their sunroom always smelled of her father's late-night cigarettes. "She's in Vancouver," she says.

I wait for more, but she just clasps her hands over her stomach like a schoolteacher at a desk.

Mr. Laptop gets up and grabs the key to the washroom off a hook.

"What about your parents?" she asks. "Do they still let you have fast food on Meeting Day?"

Just as I'm starting to wonder what I'm doing here, chitchatting about baby daddies with some long-lost neighbor, she comes up with that. How many other people in this world know about fast food on Meeting Day?

On May 12, the date my parents first took me in their arms and I became theirs, we always go out for a special Chinese meal. The only exception was when I was seven and decided that a cheeseburger and onion rings were much more celebratory. My parents had been very down on the idea, but I'd gotten quite stuck on it. I'd insisted that my feelings should count just as much as theirs, especially since it was *my* day. Then, at the last minute, I'd invited Bev along, despite knowing full well the occasion was really meant for the three of us and the three of us alone.

Bev's smile widens, like she knows she's got me. Though her teeth are straight now, I notice her grin is still a little crooked.

"Just that one time," I say. "My dad had a bypass two years ago and now my mom won't let him eat anything but sprouts."

Bev looks a little disappointed. "Is he good now?"

"Yeah," I say. "He's fitter than ever."

The purse at Bev's feet begins to ring. She reaches down with a grunt and starts piling things on the wobbly table—a keychain in the shape of lips, a lighter covered in yellow happy faces, a brush full of her blond hair, a hoop earring, an ultrasound image. She finds her phone just in time for Mr. Laptop to reappear, rubbing his wet hands on his pants.

"Bev here," she says. Then, "Okay already." Then, louder, "*Okay*."

The place has gotten more crowded, and the espresso machine is running like a dojo full of karate students doing the dragon breath. Mr. Laptop will have to struggle to eavesdrop.

"I have to go," she says.

It takes me a moment to process that she's hung up and is talking to me. She's already putting stuff back in her purse. "Weird, eh?"

I'm still confused. She shoves the ultrasound image across the table to me. "It looks like a little alien, don't you think?"

She reaches for her abandoned coffee and chugs it like a thirsty marathoner, then plunks the cup down in front of me. "That's what I call it. The Little Alien."

Her purse is already slung over her shoulder. "I'm really sorry. I'll be in touch."

She's already walking away when I notice the image, The Little Alien, still on the table. I stand up and wave it over my head like a surrender flag. "Hey!"

She's already out the door. "It's okay. I've got another one," she calls back to me.

The busy girl places an apple fritter in front of Mr. Laptop, and we all watch Bev's soft, round backside disappear into the pelting snow. I look down at the near-empty cup and wonder how much caffeine she and her baby just drank.

By the time I get home, my father is back from the university and busy grading first-year papers, a defeated scowl on his face.

"I hate my life," he says. "How are you?" Then he dives right back in, as if torturing himself is far more important than actually waiting for a reply from his daughter. I gladly leave him to it so I can go up to my room and commune with my laptop in peace.

My father will not let me get a smart phone—he says as soon as I turn eighteen, I'm perfectly welcome to buy my own way into the "distracted generation." Still, I've checked for a message from Sasha exactly eight times per day since he went back to Belarus five months ago, which I know is totally OCD. At least it doesn't have to be at the same time every day, which would really interfere with my life and become "an issue." As always, there is no message. *Zilch, nada, bupkis.*

I look around for the wooden step stool I've had since forever. My mother hand-painted my name on it in Chinese characters that look like crushed spiders. It's gone, which means my father probably stole it to change a lightbulb, and I have no choice but to open the bottom drawer of my dresser and use it as a step.

On the top shelf of my closet are two boxes stacked one on top of the other. They are exactly the same, except the top one is kind of tattered and the bottom one is pristine. They're made of creamy cardboard covered in red poppies with swirling stems so thin you can hardly see them. At one time, these boxes held silk robes that now hang in our house, spread-eagled on curtain rods. The black robe is in my parents' bedroom and the turquoise one is in mine. Both robes are embroidered all over with gold lotus flowers. Smiling silver dragons wind their way up toward the collar, as if their silky pink tongues want to whisper a secret in your ear.

I reach up and across the closet, clutching an empty hanger for balance. The bottom box is jutting out a tiny bit, and I've just managed to grab it when the drawer slides and I go down.

A mound of discarded clothes breaks my fall, but my right elbow slams into an open spot of hardwood. It hurts enough to make me cry, but I don't. There's a familiar *creak* at the bottom of the stairs and I know my mother is home. When my father is concentrating, he wouldn't notice if a submarine crashed into the den. There's another *creak*, and another, then nothing.

Our house is a hundred years old, with cracks in every corner like crow's feet. It's as if it's seen too much to let anyone get away with anything. So I know my mother is trying to stand gingerly on the third step, all five feet ten inches of her, tall for a Polish woman, not wanting to interfere because my door is closed but wondering if I've broken my neck.

"You okay up there?"

My mother could reach those boxes in my closet without a step stool but wouldn't dream of it because she believes everyone has a right to her own private space.

"All good," I shout.

But maybe I'm a little too quick to respond or maybe she can actually hear, from midway up the stairs, blood racing to my throbbing elbow. Either way, she's at my door with amazing speed for a middle-aged journalist who smoked a pack a day in her twenties and could stand to lose forty pounds. She's waded through the clutter on the floor and is hunkered down beside me before I can think of an explanation.

She touches the pristine box at my feet, then strokes my cheek with her generous sausage-like fingers. "Haven't had that down for a while, eh?"

I nod, afraid that if I speak I'll start bawling and never stop. I've been told that even as a toddler, the only time I cried was when I'd hurt myself. I've wondered sometimes if my mother is the same about sentiment. A hard-nosed realist in all other aspects of her life, she becomes a blubbering softie with me. When she talks about becoming a mother at forty-two, she cries. When she talks about how brave my birth mother was, how she risked severe punishment by leaving me in a busy market so I would be discovered quickly, she cries. When we get together with other families like ours, a bunch of spoiled Chinese girls and their doting, bleary-eyed Caucasian parents, she cries. Faster than most kids, I learned that weeping could mean happiness. I trusted everything she said about the adoption, everything she felt, because my mother couldn't fake that kind of thing if she tried.

She's mistaken about the box though. It's not the one she thinks it is. The worn one we must've opened up and gone through a hundred times when I was a kid is still in the closet.

"You want to talk?" she asks. "I can't believe it's been so long."

With her settled there on her haunches in khakis and a baggy white blouse, I get a glimpse of her peasant ancestors—she could be crouching in a wheatfield, ready to lunch on a hunk of cheese and a sauerkraut bun.

I just want her to leave so I can get some ice for my elbow.

"I'm good," I say. "I just got the urge, for some reason."

This seems to satisfy her. She pats my knee, struggles to her feet with all the grace of a big-boned, out-of-shape reporter and stares dreamily into the middle distance. "I swear you used to sleep with that thing." Then she heads off to try and reach some city councilor for a comment on something.

I pull the sonogram out of my jeans pocket and get on my knees as if about to pray at an altar of dirty laundry. I smooth out the image on top of the box and trace the shadowy white form with my finger. You can make out maybe a couple of ribs, a strangely oblong skull, spindly insect legs. It looks so ugly, so black and white, so *scientific* against the creamy cardboard and painted flowers.

I find a pen under an old Shakespeare essay that made my father proclaim me some kind of prodigy in the critical arts. On the back of the image I write, *She calls it the Little Alien.* Then I shove it into the pristine box, which is empty except for another black-and-white picture, also procured on the sly while with a childhood friend and that will also haunt my dreams if I let it.

I check my posts and messages, then go downstairs and steal one of the cold packs my mother uses when her back goes out. When I was little, I actually pictured her spine going out for the day, maybe doing a little shopping, so my mother had to either stay in bed or slither around like a snake.

Back in my room, I nurse my elbow and eat some sugar snap peas from a bag that says they were "best before" yesterday. My phone buzzes, and I know it's my best friend, Celeste, because she always gets antsy around this time, anxious to firm up her plans for the night. But it's not Celeste.

R U there?

I don't remember giving Bev my number at the coffee shop. Out of the blue, though, I remember that when we were kids, she liked to throw out stupid challenges, just for kicks. "Let's see who can go without peeing the longest," or "Let's pull each other's hair and see who screams first." And I remember the day she moved away.

Bev was standing in her driveway, surrounded by boxes, watching my father struggle to get my cello case into the hatchback. She was wearing a black tank top that said *Sweetie Pie* in purple glitter, and she had straightened her thin blond hair, like always, because her hair grew slowly and she thought it added length. We didn't speak that day, hadn't spoken in months, but I remember her smirking at no one in particular, all alone among the assorted movers and half siblings, because Bev always seemed alone even when that house was full of people.

Fast-forward about a decade—what kind of person gives a sonogram of their unborn child to someone they barely know anymore?

There's another buzz. Change of plans. C off 2nite. R U up 4 a flick with us? Come on, Faye, baby. Three's a thrill...C

The thought of tagging along with Celeste and her beefy, worshipful boyfriend Carson is almost as painful as my elbow.

I ignore Celeste and reply to Bev. Yes.

I reach under the white eyelet bed skirt I thought was the height of chic when I was twelve and pull out Sasha's sweatshirt. I press it to my face and inhale like my life depends on the scent of cheap orange candies and cigarettes. Though I know it's ridiculous, I think of this Confucian poem I used to love, the one I would recite in both Mandarin and English for the delight of my parents. But later on, in my bed, it was just for me.

Through the cloud and gloom I was
Your constant star

Now you have gone from sight
And love's white star
Roams aimless through
The night.

I'd whisper it to myself, first in one language, then the other, trying to imagine what it must be like to love someone like that.

My parents, like all good Westerners who adopt from China, fed me this stuff like it was spinach. For the first five years of elementary school, I studied Mandarin every Saturday morning. We faithfully celebrated every Chinese ritual and occasion with the other white and yellow blended families in town. We flew across the country to celebrate Chinese New Year with my oldest friend, Emma, whom we think I shared a crib with at the orphanage. But even that wasn't enough, not for my keener parents. A year ago, they splurged on a two-week extravaganza in the southern rice paddies and the stinking hot Chinese city where I was abandoned.

My phone rings and I'm startled, as if I'd just wandered into some ancient brushstroke painting where nothing as profane as technology dared exist.

"Faye," Bev shouts, "is that you?"

I hold the phone a few inches away and try to catch my breath. "Yeah."

"I am so sorry for bailing on you like that," she gushes. "I won't go into it because it's too depressing. But it was fantastic to see you again and I was wondering if you still wanted to get together, talk about old times. I still remember your house, with that old piano and everything. I'd love to see it again, just for fun, because I still remember it, you know?"

In my memory, we were almost always at Bev's house. It didn't matter if I came home ready to puke up a bag of colored marshmallows or with permanent-marker tattoos covering my thighs—my parents always let me go back there. Until they didn't.

"Sure," I say. "Yeah."

"Does your dad still mow the grass in sweat socks and sandals and that big straw hat? Your dad was so adorable. Mr. Crazy Professor."

There was a time when I worshipped my father. I thought he was the cleverest man in the world and would jump through hoops like a trained doggie just to please him. I wonder what he would say now if he knew I was inviting Bev Novak over and that she remembered him as a giant dork.

"Yeah," I say. "He still burns easily and he's still crazy."

There's a *creak* on the stairs, the bouncy gait of the man himself, a post-surgery marathoner who's fit as a fiddle. "Supper's on. Couscous with mango and prawns."

"Can I call you back?" I say.

There's another text from Celeste. Have U gone AWOL on me? U have to come out sometime, or I will hunt U down.

I press the sweatshirt to my face, take one last good hit and think of the story that's in all the Buddhist picture books for kids. The details are always different, but the gist is the same. A man wins a small lottery and buys himself a horse. The villagers all say, "What good luck!" But the man's father says, "Perhaps, perhaps not." Not long after that, the man falls off his horse and breaks his leg. The villagers all say, "What bad luck!" But the man's father says, "Perhaps, perhaps not." Then one day a war breaks out, and the army comes recruiting. The man is too lame and so escapes the bloodshed that follows.

Interesting how I think of this right after my little accident with the drawer, because since when was I such a daredevil? My careful, anal nature is a family joke. I was a clean freak before I could walk, which I didn't bother with until I was nearly two. There's video of me crawling around picking up my father's lost pens, lone socks, bits of dried-up cereal, you name it, and returning them to their rightful places.

It wasn't until very recently that I started letting things scatter and pile up on my bedroom floor like garbage in the wind. Is this disgusting? Perhaps, perhaps not. Isn't it a good thing that the dirty clothes cushioned my fall?

Perhaps, perhaps not. I do know it's freaking out my mother, though she would never admit it.

"Get it while it's hot," my father calls.

I shove Sasha's sweatshirt deep beneath my bed and stare at my phone. Maybe the more you have to hide, the more appealing mess becomes.

How bout tomorrow nite? I text Bev. After 7? U remember the address?

After Bev hightailed it out of the coffee shop today, Mr. Laptop's gaze fixed on me. It was like last year back in China, when people on the street stared openly. Sometimes they would point at me but address my parents, as if I had no voice of my own. "She Chinese?"

"Yes, yes," my parents would say reassuringly in their lousy practiced Chinese. "She's our daughter, but she was born here, in Guangzhou."

Most nodded approvingly, and a few remained confused. Either way, I came to loathe it.

Bev texts right back, as if she's been sitting there strumming her fingers on that big belly, waiting. Yes and yes.

In the coffee shop, I'd shoved the Little Alien into my pocket, away from prying eyes.

I wish now that I'd had the guts to stare down Mr. Laptop and his nosy, judgmental gaze with my dutiful almond eyes.

I wish he'd scalded his tongue on his mediocre micro-wave pastry.

I wish there'd been some kind of surge in the outlets so that when he finally got back to work, he'd been greeted by the blue screen of death.

TWO

Before lunch the next morning, Celeste shows up at our door. "I've got the truck. You have no choice, my dear. Get in quietly and I won't make a fuss."

My mother shoos me out the door like I'm a sickly kid who needs fresh air, and Celeste gives her a mock salute. "Leave her to me, ma'am."

Celeste is very good at most things, including giving off an easy, respectful confidence adults find reassuring. The only exception I can think of is our French teacher, Mme. Martin, who has some kind of chip on her shoulder when it comes to smart young women.

Outside, the sun is glaring and the March ugliness is on full display. The snowbanks are coated in grit and sand. It's been so long since the giant elms on our boulevard made a cozy arch of green, it's easy to believe they'll stay gray and dark forever. The side streets are covered in snow that's melted and then frozen again into tire-chewing ruts. But Celeste is unfazed; she drives with the same steadiness she always does.

"So what's with you?" she asks. "You not answering your phone?"

When I don't reply right away, she knocks on my head with her knuckles. "Hello? Are you there?"

I bat her hand away, and the truck swerves a little toward the curb. For some reason, this makes me laugh. "Hands on the wheel," I say.

She's like a dog with a bone though. She will not move on until she's dug up an explanation.

"Nothing's with me," I say. "I'm just enjoying doing nothing."

But this is obviously not enough.

"Is it about Kyle?"

This is truly laughable, but I don't dare, because Celeste takes it very seriously when she tries to fix me up. Last month it was, "Okay, he's really into music, and he does karate, and Carson says he's really into Asian girls."

She always says this last part as if she's half joking and half thinking it should seal the deal. The first time she came inside my house, she said, "You're more Chinese than the Chinese," which is sort of true, but which I found strangely irritating. Who was Celeste to make smart remarks?

Celeste is Métis, about as native to Canada as it gets without being full-blooded Aboriginal. Her great-great-grandparents settled the traplines and the trade routes but don't have much to show for it now. Celeste plays the fiddle, and her sisters created their own "dirty jig." But all in all, the Métis are the big historic losers—they're just now getting a bit of land back—and their biggest cultural pursuit is arguing over who gets to be Métis.

She always speaks about these "set-ups" as if I don't see these losers every day at school. I already knew Kyle liked to talk about obscure bands. I knew he had great abs. There was nothing wrong with Kyle. I even let her talk me into thinking I was interested. I actually imagined he and I getting all sweaty at the dojo together. He'd come in close behind me and position my arms just so, breathe against my neck and say, "This is a defensive position. Keep the hands high and they can't get your eyes." Maybe he'd see me as one of those classical pin-up babes who sell out concert halls. He'd ask me to play my cello for him, swaying and sexy, in just my underwear.

But then he got back together with his old girlfriend, who is busty and freckled.

"Kyle and Sara belong together," I say to Celeste. "They kind of look alike."

Celeste looks at me with pity now, which is hard to take. I hated karate class. I hated the jumping jacks, the group yelling, the stupid air punching. Words cannot express how much this isn't about Kyle.

"Think about it," I say. "Thin lips, pointy nose. There's something ferret-like about both of them."

Celeste keeps her eyes on the road. "When did you get so nasty?"

"What's wrong with ferrets?" I ask.

She shakes her head, but I can tell she's ready to let it drop. She's ready to let things become normal and easy between us again. "No wonder you never get lucky," she says.

At the mall, she tries on jeans, and every pair is tailor-made for her athletic perfection. I try to convey the right amount of enthusiasm without crossing the line into insincerity.

She asks what I'm doing tonight, and I tell her Emma is flying in tomorrow.

"Your old orphanage buddy?" she shouts from the change room. They've met before, and she pretended to like Emma until finally pronouncing her "a tremendous geek with Toronto pretensions," which is true enough. I tell her yes, that Emma.

"So what?" she shouts. "That's tomorrow."

I lie with alarming ease. "I need to tidy up. Wash the sheets and stuff."

Celeste manages to open the curtain with an armful of jeans and hands full of hangers. She dumps them on a chair meant for loyal boyfriends.

"You're the queen of anal," she says. "The absolute queen."

Celeste has a part-time job at a grocery store. She has a driver's license. She has the marks for med school but wants to be a politician of all things, like her father. There are times when she makes me feel as immature as I look, and yet I know there are some things she will never understand.

★ ✱ ★

Before Bev arrives, my parents leave for their first curling game, which they find too cute for words. They are wearing overpriced vintage curling sweaters that someone's grandma knit forty years ago, and they traipse off ready for an evening of ironic detachment.

"As a Scottish Canadian, I've let down my people sorely over the years," my father says. "But as God is my witness, that ends tonight."

People curl every day, but my father must turn it into a farcical return to his roots. I wonder what would happen to his self-satisfied grin if I told him Bev Novak would be arriving soon with her unwanted, unborn kid.

When she comes to the door, her nose is extra pink from the cold, and with her hair in pigtails, she looks like an adorable cocker spaniel. She's wearing a plum-colored parka that barely clears her waist. It couldn't be done up if she tried, and I wonder if it's possible for a baby to feel cold in the womb.

She kicks off her untied runners and squeezes past me. Hands still in her parka pockets, she walks right in. "Still the same," she says.

I follow her into the front hall, where she spins around slowly in her sock feet. Some pregnant women look like they've swallowed a beach ball, but not Bev—every inch of her is just a little more round.

"The same," she says again.

This seems to please her, but I feel the need to point some things out. "All those bookshelves are built right into the walls now, and everything's a shade darker. And the stairs aren't painted anymore. We stripped it off. It's all natural oak now."

She crinkles her nose. "Really?"

Before I can say, *Really, I sucked in dust and fumes for weeks,* she takes off into the living room. "Green walls," she says, "and a million books, that's what I remember. That's the same."

She picks up a lacquered box from the coffee table. My father got it for my mother the Christmas they decided to adopt from China. It's egg-shaped and glossy black, with tiny shards of inlaid pearl in the shape of a bird.

"This used to be somewhere else," Bev says. She looks around. "Like on the piano or something. I remember thinking a flamingo should not be white."

As far as I know, our piano has always been covered in family photos, but I couldn't say for sure. "It's a whooping crane," I say.

She laughs like I've made a joke and carefully puts the box back in exactly the same place. "Remember when we almost broke it?"

I shake my head. "When?"

But she's already on to something else. For maybe twenty minutes, she pokes around, keeping up a running commentary as if the whole point of her being here is to tour the house. She points at the wall over the loveseat and squeals in delight. "That painting!"

She kneels on the cushions and fingers the scroll, tracing the Chinese characters as if they're braille. "I used to wish I looked just like her."

It's a relatively simple piece. The scroll isn't covered with intricate birds or meaningful leaves or mountains rising gloriously in the distance. There's just a woman in a flowing robe, holding a fan over her shoulder. She is willowy, with sad, delicate features and black hair piled up on her head like scoops of ice cream. For years, I liked to imagine that she was my birth mother.

Bev shoves down the waistband of her leggings and reveals three Chinese characters tattooed in the small of her back. "I got this two years ago. I had to forge Lara's signature."

I need to think for a moment to remember who Lara is—Bev's mother, Lara, the only mother on the street who didn't have a job. Who was never in-between—either laughing or crying, in our way or holed up in her room, fat or skinny. The only thing that never changed was her gorgeousness.

"Did it hurt?" I ask.

She shrugs. "'Beauty plus strength equals woman.' That's what it says."

Though I never made great strides with written Chinese, I'm skeptical. I straighten the scroll, even though it's not crooked. "She's a prostitute," I say. "Tang Yin, the artist, loved to paint ladies of ill repute. The poem on the side is about how hypocritical people are."

Bev claps her hands and laughs as if I've just performed a clever trick. "Well, I guess I always did have big dreams for myself, didn't I!"

I don't mention that I haven't actually read a whole translation of the poem, just a little about Tang Yin, how he liked to depict outward calm and inward pain, so he painted a lot of prostitutes.

Bev wobbles a bit and has to grab the arm of the loveseat.

"You okay?" I ask.

She shrugs again. "I should probably eat something. I never feel like it and then I forget."

In the kitchen, she opens the fridge and makes a face. "Does your mom still drink that stuff?"

I look at the row of shiny pink cans as if seeing them for the first time. It seems my mother has been addicted to diet grapefruit soda for over ten years.

"Remember she didn't let you drink it because of the chemicals," Bev says, "and I dared you to sneak one and down it in the basement? You were such a sweetie pie though. Daddy's little girl."

I don't mention my longstanding fear of our cellar-like basement full of spiders and broken furniture. She cracks open a can and chugs, then wipes her mouth with her parka sleeve. "And that time when your dad gave us stalks of rhubarb and told us to lie down on the grass so he could put the sugar for dipping in our belly buttons? And you believed him?"

I have no memory of Bev being in our leafy backyard. In my mind, we were always at her place, sitting on the roof of their toolshed, pointlessly shouting at joggers as they huffed down the lane on a perfect summer morning. "Hey, mister, your fly's undone!"

"Oh"—Bev groans—"and your dad's nachos. Those were the best ever. I still hate black olives, but I totally loved them on those nachos."

When did my father ever make Mexican for Bev?

"I could totally go for those nachos," Bev says.

"My mother's banned all chips and sour cream," I say.

Her lips have gone almost as pale as her face, and she's using the fridge to hold herself up.

"What about yogurt?" I ask. "We've got the high-protein Balkan kind."

By the time she sits down with a spoon at the kitchen table, I swear she's ready to pass out. She starts shoveling in peach-mango yogurt like a robot programmed to open and close its mouth every 2.5 seconds.

"So where did you move?" I ask. "I mean, back then. I don't even know."

She talks between spoonfuls like there's nothing to it. Swallow, speak, swallow, speak, repeat. "After my dad sold the restaurants, we went to Sarnia. Then I went with Lara to Vancouver. Then Ray came back here last year, and so did I."

I remember there were always leftover desserts at her house—day-old cheesecakes and mixed-berry pies—and her father, Ray, left a satisfying scent of cooking oil and cigarettes and vanilla.

I try not to stare at her stomach. It's hard to believe skin can expand like that, stretchy as Silly Putty. "Whereabouts are you?" I ask. "What school?"

She finally pauses, turning the spoon over on her tongue as if to ensure that every last bit is consumed. "Doing correspondence. With the move and everything, it seemed stupid to start somewhere new for my last year."

"Right," I say, like I talk to people doing high school by correspondence every day.

She leans back in the chair and groans, resting her hands on her belly. She lets her head drop back, but her lips have regained some of their adorable pinkness. She waves her hand in a square, following the crown molding around the ceiling. "We had that in our old house too. Then Lara took it down because she was all into clean lines. She still talks about it. She says going all modern was the beginning of the end."

I don't know what to say to this. I remember the day Lara's new egg-shaped coffee table was delivered and we spent a happy half hour pressing our faces into the glass, imprinting every inch with kisses and nostril marks.

She lifts her head and smiles her slightly crooked grin. "Remember that glass coffee table?"

Pregnant Bev Novak, groaning in my parents' kitchen chair, has read my mind. "I remember the mess we made of it," I say.

She laughs, and her belly moves with her. "It busted in the moving van. And not into just a few pieces. A million pieces."

My phone buzzes, and I act like I have no choice but to check it out.

Hey, birth buddy. Weather news, plse. Rubber or fur? To-do list: cool toy store by museum, Greek place with gravy/fries, vintage. Bringing surprise. Hint: green hair, schoolboy tie. Flight 134 from TO arrives 4:12 pm, your time. TTFN...Em/Liang

"Excuse me a sec," I say, but Bev has already gotten up and is nosing around the dining room.

I sneak upstairs and check my messages for the first time since this morning. My doctor has said that OCD symptoms are exacerbated by stress. I stand for a moment in the dim quiet, with nothing but the familiar hum of the computer hardware, and try to collect my thoughts.

"You still play this?" Bev shouts.

I come down and she's pointing at the hulking black case in the corner. Twice I've moved the cello case from that corner onto the back porch, and twice my father has put it back. "Not for a while," I say.

I remember the one and only time I played my cello for her. I was eight, and my latest big accomplishment was Gounod's *Meditation on Ave Maria*. We were outside on the front porch, and the acoustics of the breezeless evening weren't bad. For once, she was speechless.

"So?" I had asked.

She looked at me as if I'd just pulled a rabbit out of a hat. "I didn't know you could do that."

I shrugged. "I want to quit. It's boring."

"Shut up," she said. "You're a crappy liar. Play something else."

Now, she cocks her head and looks disappointed, like when I told her about my father's heart scare. "Really? You quit? You're lying."

I can't tell if she's trying to mock or flatter me. She sounds so sincere, as if she's going to say something like *You should never give up on your dreams.* I tell her what I've basically been telling everybody. "I guess I just needed a break."

She nods, having already moved on to examining the Scottish teacups my father inherited when his mother died. "They're a little twee for us," my mother had said, but she'd put them on display anyway.

"Listen," I say. "I'm sorry, but my mom just puked at work and she needs me to pick her up."

Bev finishes off the last of the soda and holds her hands up like she's about to dance. "Hey, no problem. I should get going anyway."

I silently plead with her not to ask for a ride. "Sorry," I say.

"No problem, Faye," she says, handing me the can. She pretends to try to do up her parka zipper and laughs at her own joke. "You guys always were three little peas in a pod."

The cab company is on her speed dial. She gives them the address of her old house across the street, then has to correct herself. "It's the Little Alien," she whispers to me. "It's stealing my brain cells."

Her arms are around me before I know what's happening. "Thanks for the refreshments. I'll be in touch. Winnipeg is such a great place to raise a kid. We know that, eh?"

She's out the door before I can answer. There's no way the cab is even on its way yet, but I let her go. I let her go stand out on the sidewalk in the frigid spring night, or walk to the corner, or whatever her plan is, because I don't know how to stop her.

I don't want to stop her.

Alone in my bedroom, I shove my face into Sasha's sweatshirt and inhale. This scent, his scent, usually brings back *the night*, but really, I'd smelled him long before that. Like in the school band, where I played the flute and he pretended to.

I tell myself our story, from the beginning, for the thousandth time, because I have borderline OCD and because I don't want to imagine where Bev and her belly are.

Sasha showed up in September, the beginning of school, but rarely came to class. When he did, he would slouch in a few minutes late and park his conspicuous six-foot-three-inch frame in a chair behind me. He always sucked on one of those hard citrus candies that are wrapped in cellophane, the kind a restaurant might hand out with your bill. He'd quietly assemble his flute and then pretend to join in with whatever we were playing.

As lead flautist, I should have got to the bottom of it, but what could I have done? What would have been the point in confronting the exchange student who probably didn't even know how foreign he really looked in the middle of the girlie instrument section? Now and then, when someone wasn't quick enough to look away, he would smile, showing off his silver tooth, and nod formally, as if to say, *Good day to you, miss.* Celeste dubbed him the Freaky Russian and dismissed him with "nice long legs, nice blue eyes, shame about the bad teeth and general weirdness." I pretended not to notice that, miraculously, he could suck candy and maintain his embouchure at the same time. Whether he noticed *me*, or even gave me a second thought in those lead-up weeks, is unclear.

Cut to *the night.* For the band trip in November, I'm billeted with a nice enough jock named Hannah, who's obsessed with skiing in some future Olympics and whose sprawling Calgary bungalow is covered in cat hair. We go to a party at another sprawling Calgary bungalow, somewhere in the foothills. Celeste is not there. She's in Winnipeg and has no say in what I do or don't do. She is not there to tell anyone who will listen that if you can't have a good time without alcohol, she feels totally sorry for you.

It's unclear who gives me the first beer. The fat percussionist who is hosting, or someone I know from school? It is a light amber lager with snow-covered mountains on the label. It's unclear whether I finish three bottles or four. Or what makes me go outside—the bloated feeling or the spinning feeling? I close my eyes and watch the stars do their little dance.

There are others outside, mostly smokers, scattered in small groups around a vast backyard pool that's been covered for the winter. I find a dark corner where a faulty solar light has failed. I lean against the edge of a waterless concrete fountain to get my balance. I breathe in the mountain air, cool and yet unusually warm for this time of year.

"You no smoke?"

He appears out of the darkness, a slouched outline, dim except for the orange glow of the cigarette hanging from his lips.

I shake my head.

The glow grows stronger for a moment before it's sent flying into the yellow November grass. He looks down at his feet. "Is good. My father smoke and smoke and then lung cancer. That's it. But that is Russians. We smoke, smoke, drink, drink, and we don't live too long."

The Freaky Russian is speaking to me like we're old friends. It's like I can feel the world spinning on its axis. I hug myself in the chill, but my insides burn. My voice is hardly my own. "I'm sorry. About your father."

He looks up and shrugs. I can't make out real color, but there are contrasts in his face. Dark lips. Light eyes. "This happens."

I nod, like I have a clue.

He grins, reaches out for my arm, and his hands feel very big and very hot. "You cold? You want to walk? To go?"

Then we're walking through the suburban quiet, warming ourselves with the small bottle of whiskey in his pocket. He asks if I'm Chinese, if I'm China-born, and I explain it to him for what seems like forever. It's unclear exactly what I say.

"Ahh," he says, "you are a foundling."

This makes me laugh. It sounds like something out of a fairytale.

"What?" he asks. "Is this not right? Foundling?"

To talk and walk with me, he must not so much slouch as bend. I am laughing so hard I'm afraid I might pee. Now and then, he holds on to my elbow and we hold each other up.

"So what's with your flute playing?" I ask, because I am suddenly fearless.

He stops and straightens, then grins down at me. His eyetooth gleams under the streetlight. "You know my secret, yes? You know why I do it? Joan, my church lady who sponsor me, she ask if I read music. Why? I ask. She say I can go to the Rocky Mountains with the school. I tell her, yes, of course. I see at the church there is a flute. I tell her the flute. So here I am."

I'm laughing again. "Was it worth it?"

"No!" he shouts, joining me, outdoing me, in his laughter. "*Nyet*. My home, it is dull, it is poor farms, poor factories, it is shit. I think, give me the wild Canada mountains. But now not so much. The day before, the sights are beautiful, but then I feel like they are too close, too big. How you say? Dungeon? Like a dungeon."

Never before have I met someone who doesn't dig the mountains. I tell him something I've never told anyone. I tell him I felt the same way in China, that the magnificently rising steppes and moving walls of people were suffocating.

He wipes his nose on his sleeve and waves dismis-sively. "And this rich place. These houses, all the same. I hate them, and I want them. They are, how you say— they are a contradiction for me."

Then he takes my arm and guides me to a wrought-iron bench placed in a circle of gravel on someone's front lawn.

"What a moronic place for a seat," I say. "Who's going to sit out here watching traffic?"

He ignores me. He puts his hand on my thigh, and I both like it and do not like it. He offers me more whiskey, and I take a long, hot drink. "It's good to sit," he says. "I see you now. I see your face."

The world turns on its axis again and we are kissing. Our breath is steamy in the night air, and his hands move across my back, my stomach, my cheeks, like he's a blind man trying to see me. Never before has it felt like this. I am not going through the motions. There is no vague sense of letdown even as it's happening.

Now and then he stops and grins like he did in band class. "Is good?" he asks. "Okay?"

"Is good," I say.

"This bench," he finally says. "This bench is no good." He whispers the words into my neck, just below the earlobe. "We go somewhere. Somewhere different."

But it's too late. The hard moronic bench is enough to break the spell, and I'm pulling away, like always. "I should go. My ride will be wondering where I am."

He pulls his sweatshirt over his head and I glimpse the crop of shiny blond hair around his belly button. "No, no," he says. "Is good." I let him wrap me up and pull me toward him. "Like this then," he says. "Like this a little longer. Is good, no?"

I drop my head onto his chest, and his T-shirt is so thin that I can feel each individual rib.

"You are a little bird," he says. "I have to hold, or *flit, flit*, you fly."

I laugh, kiss him before he can say anything else. It is so, so good, our tongues hot in the cold night, just like this, going nowhere.

Until we have no choice—we must walk together across the dead, manicured lawn, past the cookie-cutter dream homes, past the police cruisers shutting down the party and then separately onto a plane crowded with hungover band students who are one minute of turbulence away from mass vomiting.

Now, I hear my parents coming in the door, eager to share their zany middle-class night of curling.

Maybe perfect Celeste is right. I'm getting nasty. I keep things from her—like Sasha, like Bev—and I don't know why exactly. Just for kicks, maybe. Or take annoying Emma.

She's the closest link to my birthplace I'm ever going to get, and I wish I never had to see her again. Or my smug, oh-so-doting parents, who only want the best for me—I'd rather get a cavity filled or drink one of those hideous diet sodas Bev poisoned her fetus with earlier than talk to them right now.

I lied to Bev for no particular reason, except that I suddenly wanted to be alone with a cheap poly-blend sweatshirt and my borderline OCD. I just wanted to sit here, on my cesspool of a bedroom floor, with the Chinese robe on my wall looming over it all.

Only its silver embroidered dragon is no longer smiling at me like it used to. Now it's laughing.

tHREE

For the first eight months of my life, my name was Xiao Shang Chang and Emma's was Xiao Jin Liang. Now and then, you hear of some Chinese orphanages giving their tiny charges flowery names like Bright Lotus and Tender Blossom. But whoever was in charge of handing them out at the Nanning Center for Infants and Children didn't believe in sugarcoating things. We were Miss Market and Miss Bridge, in honor of where we were found.

Our parents love to tell stories about the two of us as babies. On the flight home from China, Emma was moonfaced and sleepy. I was bony and alert. She charmed the entire plane, seeming to say her new name over and over—"Amma, amma, amma." I wailed pretty much the whole time, which my parents saw as a sign that I'd bonded with my orphanage caregiver and so was behaving in a healthy and appropriate manner given the situation.

Now, sixteen years later when Emma comes down the escalator at the airport, she's holding two eerily life-like Japanese dolls in her arms. The male is dressed like the leader of a boy band and the girl looks like any teenage hipster you'd see in any major city in the world.

"May I present Lily and Yashiro," Emma says to my father and me. "Don't ask how much they cost."

Years ago, I realized that Emma is beyond mockery or irony. Even when visiting me and my atheist parents, she's never shy about saying her own grace before meals. She struts around in her one-piece bathing suit at the pool like she has no idea she's fat. She is the only person I know with less sexual experience than me, and she doesn't seem to care.

On the ride home, she tells us that Yashiro cost over eight hundred dollars, and though he looks quite feminine with his fine features and elaborately coiffed hair, he is all man. She tells us she's just received a full scholarship to Queen's, so her parents kicked in three hundred for Lily. She tells us Yashiro's suit was hand-sewn by a London tailor.

I can't help thinking of the pictures I've seen from the 1960s, during the height of China's communist fervor. Men and women wore the same androgynous uniform:

shapeless rough cotton pants with a shapeless tunic on top. But when we went back last year, the women on the streets were something to behold—designer outfits with matching phones, $200 haircuts and funky, cartoonish shoes. Meanwhile, my birth mother was probably hidden away in some factory, wearing hideous pink coveralls with a matching hair cap so she could stand there, all day, every day, assembling toasters.

"Are they a couple?" I ask, and my father can't help laughing.

"Mmm, no," she says.

"Fraternal twins?" my father asks.

Emma shakes her head and goes quiet, apparently uninterested in giving them any kind of backstory.

Later on, she's unpacking what are mostly doll clothes in the spare room when she suddenly gets chatty again. "Did I tell you Colm is gay?"

I've known Emma's older brother, Colm, my whole life, and for a while I had a crush on him. When I was twelve, he seemed so exotic, with his Chinese mother's black eyes and bow-shaped lips and his Irish father's wavy hair and wide shoulders. I told myself that one day he would see that not all Asian girls were like his little sister.

"He likes some guy at the bike shop," Emma says, "but I think the guy's married, so who knows."

I don't know what to do with this information. Emma's parents didn't have the usual infertility issues of other adoptive couples. Her mother's a die-hard Christian and decided that having a second child of their own with so many unwanted girls back in China wouldn't be right. "Do your parents know?"

Emma smooths down Yashiro's funky green hair like she's petting a cat. "I'm the only one he's told."

I find myself as speechless as when Colm used to come up behind me, rest his hands on my shoulders and squeeze with brotherly affection. In all our years together, Emma's religion has always been there, hovering around, but it's never come up. I am certain, though, they are not okay with homosexuality.

"You still see that as rushing," she says, and I wonder, rushing what? Colm is rushing to assume he must be gay? It was rushing to tell her so soon? Then I figure it out. What she said was, "You still seeing that Russian?"

Because I stupidly told Emma about Sasha. Three days after *the night*, when I was still consumed, unable to focus on anything else, Emma texted me. I am bored, Chang. Tell me something interesting.

So, to loosen his hold on me, I tried to pretend he was just something to gossip about. Met someone when I went west. Sasha from Belarus. He was interesting.

"He went home," I say now.

Emma sighs like I just said I failed a big cello exam. "That is awful, Faye. A guy from church just got back from helping farmers over there, and he said the soil is full of radiation. When that explosion happened, the nuclear one in the eighties, the wind blew it all north."

I let her go on, let her tell me about cancer rates and dead fish and corrupt local councils, when all I want to do is grab Yashiro and whack her across the mouth with his stylish head.

For three days I play the happy hostess. A couple of lunches with the ol' yellow daughters/white parents gang, Winnipeg chapter. Bowling in the morning with the little kids and old ladies. An afternoon of scouring downtown vintage shops for fringed purses, Emma's latest collectible. For three nights, I try to free my Sasha from Emma's chatty clutches.

I check my messages obsessively. I go over the story, in my mind, all the way to the end.

After we got home from Calgary, three weeks went by and I didn't see him. I was relieved. I imagined him grinning expectantly at Celeste and me with the silver tooth.

I imagined the whole school blabbing about the Freaky Russian's thing with Celeste's Asian friend, Faye, the one with the big cello and tiny tits. I imagined he'd disappeared just as quickly as he had come, gone back to his screwed-up country without a word.

But one day he walked into class, late as usual. It was the first Wednesday of the month, when our after-school string quartet usually performs a few pieces for the school band. He folded himself into a chair, and I lost my fingering. We were playing Beethoven's *Sonatina in D Minor,* something I've played since I was prepubescent, but he was watching me with those sad, mocking blue eyes, and the notes became a foreign language. I heard them, but I didn't hear them. I don't remember packing up my cello. I don't remember filing out of class. All I know is I was the last to leave, and he was waiting.

He was standing just past the storage room for rental instruments, near the fire-exit door, wearing an itchy-looking gray sweater that was too short at the waist and brown corduroy pants that needed a belt. If he hadn't been slouching, I probably could've seen the blond hair around his belly button.

He stared down at his runners, which were so white they practically glowed. "Tomorrow, I go," he said, then looked up and gave a little wave with his big hand. "I fly away. Bye-bye."

I willed myself not to turn around and see if anyone was watching. "I have your sweatshirt," I said. "I mean, at home. I should have brought it. But it's at home."

He grinned.

"I mean, I could get it for you," I said.

"No, no," he said. "*Nyet*. You keep. You keep as the memento. Joan, my host family lady, she got me whole case of clothes. You keep."

I dug in my pocket for my music-notation pen, grabbed his big hand and wrote on his palm. "That's my info."

He closed his hand and put it over his heart. "*Spaceba*. I thank you." He actually made a little bow. "I will—how you say? I will keep up the touch."

"You sure you don't want your sweatshirt?" I asked.

He shook his head, patted his heart. Then he nudged my cello case with his giant glowing runner. "Your instrument. How you say it like in Canada?"

I swore I heard Celeste's voice somewhere down the hallway. "Cello," I said.

"Ah, yes," he said. "Is a melancholy instrument."

It was definitely Celeste. She was shouting something about winning a bet with Carson, and I hated her more at that moment than I ever thought it was possible to hate someone. I wanted to stay with Sasha from Belarus in this quiet dead-end corner forever.

"The Russians and the Chinamen," he said. "We like the melancholy."

The term "Chinamen" made me laugh, and he looked slightly hurt. "No," I said. "I mean, yes. They say the cello is the instrument most like the human voice."

He bowed again. "I keep up the touch. You go to your friend. She is looking for you."

Sure enough, Celeste's voice echoed off the lockers and filled the school. "Where the hell is Faye? She's supposed to meet me here."

Then Sasha walked out of my life, his new white sweat socks peeking out beneath his too-short corduroys as he went.

★ ★ ★

On the last day of spring break, a couple of hours before we can finally dump Emma off at the airport, she starts to feel bloated and gassy and I get a text from Bev.

So good to see U. Just like old times! I don't know too many people here anymore. Cause I'm shy? I know, I know, hard to believe. Little Alien is trying to break my ribs with his elbow. Have something big to ask you. Call me ASAP, K?

Emma comes out of the bathroom, glassy-eyed. "I think it's too much dairy, Chang. My lactose intolerance is flaring up."

When we were first adopted, no one would've predicted Emma would end up the sickly one. I refused a lot of Western food at first, and I can't say how many times I've heard about the day my parents first ordered in Chinese food. According to family legend, I was about a year old, in Canada maybe six weeks, and before the delivery guy was even out the door, I was crawling around and yelling, "Yum-yum! Yum-yum!" at just the smell of it.

Emma throws herself down on my bed and groans. "My stomach is a balloon of gas. Look at it. I'm pregnant."

For a second, I wonder if she's read Bev's text over my shoulder. Except I know if Emma had seen something, she wouldn't tiptoe around it—she'd throw it all out there, the worst poker player ever. I know I am stuck for another couple of hours with this groaning whale on my bed, who couldn't, or wouldn't, tell a lie to save her life, when all I want to do is find out what Bev Novak wants.

"I don't think it's the cheese, Liang," I say. "I feel sick too."

In the bathroom, I try Bev, but the call goes to voice mail. I remember that not long after she moved in across the street, we figured out we were both named after dead relatives. "That is so cool," Bev had said. "I'm named after my mom's dead sister, and you're named after your dad's dead mother. And we both like red licorice better than black."

There's a tap at the door. "You okay?" my mother asks.

"Yeah," I say. "But I might have to skip the airport. My stomach's pretty off."

The lie slips out with ease and works like a charm. I am rid of Emma with a quick hug. Chang and Liang go their separate ways for another year.

Back in the bathroom, I try Bev again, and she picks up after the first ring. My mother's downstairs in the kitchen, and I try not to sound like I'm whispering.

"It's Faye," I say. "What's up?"

"Faye," she says. "Thanks for calling. You are so great, you know. You were always Miss Manners. You always said your please and thank you; you always practiced that cello like a good girl."

I wonder if she's been drinking, but even Bev can't be that irresponsible. "So what's up?" I ask again.

"Okay, so I have something to ask you. I made up my mind about the Little Alien, and I need to pick some parents. I know it sounds super crazy, but that's what I've decided to do. I have to pick some parents. And when I think about it, I always think of you, good little Faye, even though it's been so long."

She pauses, and I wait.

"So there's going to be a meeting. That's how it works. I pick a couple and then meet with them, sort of interview them. I think Denise, my worker, forgot I'm doing correspondence, so it'll be after school. Like in a couple of weeks or so. I could give you the address and you could meet us there."

Bev thinks I can drive, because I lied when she came to my house. Only Celeste knows that I aced the written portion but failed the actual driving test—twice.

"I don't have a car," I say, as if it's only a matter of logistics.

"We can pick you up," she says. "Denise has a car. We could pick you up right at the school. No problem."

"I don't know," I say.

"Hey, no problem," she says. "You think about it. I know it's crazy, it's weird, but I just thought since we're such old friends, you know? I just keep thinking it would be cool to have you there."

I hear my father come in from the airport and listen to him bicker quietly with my mother about whether they should worry about me or not. I get off the phone as soon as I can, promising to call her back.

I let my mother put me to bed with a hot-water bottle. I wait until all is quiet except for the gentle hissing of radiators in our cranky old house. Then I get down the pristine box—using the stool this time—and take out both images, placing them beside each other on the creamy lid.

The photograph has been folded in two perfect halves and doesn't want to lie flat. I made that fold in a house as quiet as this one, before tucking the picture in my suitcase beneath my remaining clean underwear. I tell myself the story, the story no one in this world knows but me.

Three years ago at Emma's Toronto townhouse. It was July, over a hundred degrees "with humidity," just like prairie folk say it's minus thirty "with windchill." I'd never experienced heat like that before and haven't since, except in southern China, where it's like you're walking under water, your body conscious of every movement pressing through the heavy air. Apparently, I have no genetic tolerance for such weather—I wilt like a true prairie girl.

Emma was sick, her annoying summer cold having turned to something nastier, and we spent most of our time in their air-conditioned TV room. It was my last day there and Emma's mother, Lu, came down on her way to work. She handed me a coffee-table book with a look of sympathy and set down a plate of cinnamon buns. She felt Emma's cheek. We waved her away, told her we knew how to use a phone.

I don't know how much time went by before I cracked open the book. It was your typical collection of photographs, probably called something like *China: Then and Now*, stuff I'd seen a million times before. But it was like the book had a mind of its own. It fell open to page eighty-one, a full-page reproduction with the caption, *Young girls chat in a moon gate in the courtyard of a Chinese house, Beijing 1932.*

In the photo, two little girls, maybe sisters, gazed at one another through a round gate in a brick wall. The one facing me stood amidst manicured greenery, her hands clasped behind her back. She was wearing a plain silk tunic and an expression that seemed to say, *Come in if you wish, or don't—it makes no difference to me.* The other one could only be seen in partial profile: her small right ear, her silk jacket embroidered with spring bouquets, her ankle-high socks and flat slippers. Her hands were by her side, and you couldn't tell if one foot was stepping into the gate or just resting there. It looked so obviously posed—globe-shaped gate framing twin-like figures, one inside, one outside—but this was part of its magic.

I sat and studied that photo for who knows how long, losing all feeling in my butt cheeks and all sense of where I was. Until the phone rang and Emma stirred and I wanted to take the pillow and cover her round, honest, snotty face.

That night, I lay awake on the blow-up mattress at the foot of Emma's bed, licking sweat from my upper lip and listening to her parents flush the toilet, check the locks, mutter their bedtime prayers. I licked and listened, licked and listened, until there were only Emma snores and the faint *whiz* of traffic outside the sealed town-house windows. Then I walked barefoot to the kitchen, where Emma's mother had left the stove light on. I grabbed a box cutter from the craft drawer and a flattened cereal box from the recycling bin.

New townhouses do not creak, have no stories to tell, and I silently headed to the TV room, flicked on the light, went blind for a moment. I slipped the cereal box behind page eighty-one and sliced the paper as close to the spine as I could manage. My hands were calm and steady, my cut clean and straight.

When I look at it now, I can hardly bear its structured beauty. It's no wonder there are no moon gates in the West. Gates here are all business, for keeping out and letting in, but circles are not about moving back and forth. They make you want to pause and consider their endless roundness, to ponder any wonders held so perfectly within their frame—and who wants that? In the new China, they don't care about moon gates either. They knock them down to build freeways and twelve-story shopping malls and private hospitals with ultrasound machines. Worried that you're having that dreaded girl? Pay up front, ladies, and you can be rid of her before your pants are feeling too tight!

The moon-gate photograph is the opposite of the Little Alien's image, whose hazy, ill-formed shape leaves me cold. What do I tell Bev Novak? That I'm not who she thinks I am? That I'm a liar and a thief?

When I was small, I believed there was a reason for everything. I didn't pray, like Emma, but I believed, I really did, until little things began to chip away at my faith. At first, you barely notice, but it adds up until everything is messy, no matter what you do or how hard you try.

Bev is the only other person who was there for the "scissor incident." Her parents were fighting in the kitchen. Lara threw a fork at Ray's face, and we retreated to Bev's room to play hair salon. Bev loved to comb my hair and would do it for hours if I let her. "You should do shampoo commercials," she said. "Sleek and shiny is in. You should send in a headshot."

"I hate my hair," I said. It wasn't true. Looks-wise, my glossy hair has always been my greatest asset. But I was seven and feeling mean. Bev and I both knew I outclassed her—better parents, better genes, better chances, better hair—and now and then I couldn't help rubbing it in, like scratching a scab when I know it will leave a scar.

"Shut up," she said. "You do not."

"I do," I said. "There's a reason people say we all look alike. Black isn't even a color."

"Shut up," she said again. "Your hair is perfect."

"I'm allowed to hate it," I said.

She told me to sit still and came back with Lara's pinking shears, the heavy ones that were too big for our hands. She grabbed a clump of my hair and tugged, but these scissors were not meant for hair. She had to work hard, opening and closing them with both hands. Tugging. Hacking. Hurting.

I began to cry. But I did not stop her. I let her keep going. She was almost panting, with the same look on her face as Ray had had when he was dodging silverware. I just sat there, closed my eyes and took it. The tugging. The hacking. The hurting. It seemed to take forever.

"There," she said. "You happy now?"

I ran out of that house, past Lara and Ray, who didn't notice my hair or my sobs or me. I ran home to my mommy and daddy and told them what big bad Beverly had done.

FOUR

In China, spring is the season to feed the dead.

On the Saturday morning of Qingming, or, in English, Clear Bright, I dream that I'm playing Rachmaninoff's *Sonata in G Minor for Cello and Piano*. I travel with the music like I used to, my imaginary bow moving slow and silky. I drift weightless through azure sky, blown by a breeze of rising and descending notes. When it builds, forte and storming, I'm an eagle riding the gale force, wild and blissfully in control.

Then there's total silence and Sasha and I are walking in the snow under the bare trees, two lost northerners, and I stick my tongue out to catch a flake. He turns me to him, exhales orange-scented fog and pulls me to him.

"I am jealous of that snow," he says before kissing me like he's leaving forever...

There's a knock on my door. "Your dad's got pancakes on the table. He's had the cooler packed for an hour."

On the way to the cemetery, my phone rings three times, no caller ID available. When I answer, I can hear a TV in the background, someone breathing, and then they hang up.

"What's the deal?" my father says after the third call.

"Who knows?" I say. "Maybe it's a robocaller."

When we get to the cemetery, the bare trees are black gashes in the electric-blue sky, the grass nearly snowless and dead yellow.

"Welcome to Winnipeg," my father says cheerfully. "Clear and bright."

Qingming used to be my favorite festival—I loved the chilly picnic, the finger food, the crazy tribute of burning money. I even liked the orderly open rows of the graves. When Celeste questioned the whole "cooking for corpses" thing, I didn't point out that her First Nations relatives ancestor-worship with the best of them.

Last year, I looked up the origin of this "no fire" cold-food occasion, which apparently comes from a legend about an emperor and his former aide, Jie Zitui. The emperor wanted to reward the aide for his past loyalty, but the aide had become a hermit who refused all visitors except his mother. So the emperor set fire to the forest where they lived, hoping to drive them out and justly honor them but instead burning them both alive. *Henceforth, no fires shall be lit on this day,* the emperor announced, *in honor of my faithful servant, Jie Zitui.* I've never really felt the same way about Qingming since. I've forgotten my sunglasses, and there's a sharp north wind. I'm just thankful we no longer do the kite thing. For years, my parents would present me with a new Qingming kite, as is tradition, so we could get it to fly high enough that we might cut the string and watch it float up to the heavens. But mostly it would involve my father racing back and forth, tossing it aloft with all the grace of a born academic, while my mom and I watched it nose-dive as he hurled obscenities.

This time, my mother struggles just to keep the picnic blanket flat while my father happily unpacks his basketful of goodies: hunks of roast chicken and duck, hard-boiled eggs, fruit salad, iced tea. He carefully lines them up on his in-laws' graves like he's expecting a buffet crowd any second.

Kneeling awkwardly on the blanket, my mother sets up our little shrine: a framed photo of my father's parents; a small jade burner in the shape of a Buddha-like panda; the worn-out cardboard poppy box I used to cherish like a teddy bear. She places some incense in the panda's outstretched paws.

"Ah, my dear ma and pa, Scottie and Faye," my father says in his bad Scottish burr. "What a pair ye were."

My dad's parents have no graves for us to clean, since they were both cremated before I came along and their ashes thrown into the creek behind their beloved farmhouse. My father lights the incense, but he refuses to burn the money, because he says poor Scottie would've thought it a sacrilege. My father has a hard time taking any kind of ritual seriously. He claims it's because he knows ritual is both necessary and ridiculous, which is why he put the panda burner in my Christmas stocking.

My mother rests the burner on top of the poppy box and takes both of us by our icy hands. "Thank you, Chinese ancestors, for allowing us our Faye. We are forever grateful."

My father passes me the flame igniter and a twenty. It's my turn to speak, and I'm glad I don't have to think. I can just repeat the same glorious sentiment I came up with when I was ten. "Thank you for life. Thank you for this life. May I make you proud with all that I've been given."

My father kisses me on the top of my head, and when I squeeze my mother's hand, she seems so grateful it's pathetic. She places some red carnations by each of her parent's headstones, then lights up another twenty. She is always quiet when it's her turn, as if she's not willing to share what this charade might mean to her or to her parents, two devout Catholics who died with last rites. They're probably rolling in their graves as the money turns to swirling black smoke in the wind.

I force myself to eat some duck, but the fruit salad is practically frozen and we agree to save it for later. When we get home, my father presents me with a hand-painted kite in the shape of a dragonfly. He spied it in Chinatown on his last trip to Vancouver and couldn't resist. "I thought you could hang it from your ceiling. It's got most of your colors."

It is truly beautiful, a work of art, but all I can think of is having those bulgy insect eyes staring down at me as I sleep.

That night my phone rings twice more, caller ID unavailable. The second time, there's a male voice. "Who is this?"

"Who is *this*?" I ask, and he hangs up.

Afterward, I dream I'm playing Tchaikovsky's *Valse Sentimental*, my fingers flying over the strings like sparrows flitting from branch to branch, when all goes silent, and Sasha and I are walking along our back lane. It's summer, and garbage cans fill the air with a putrid sweetness, but we don't care because we only smell each other. He bends his great height like a young tree in a gale-force wind and picks up a seashell.

"Shhh," he says and holds it to my ear. I obediently listen to the primordial churning while he whispers sweet nothings into my neck.

★*★

At school on Monday, I do my best to fly beneath the radar. Carson is getting clingy, and Celeste mostly wants to plan out her next move. I respond to every text but beg off anything more, feigning further stomach trouble. I check my messages. Though it's been over a week since we talked, I do not call Bev.

On Tuesday, my mother decides we should "do lunch."

"I'll pick you up at school," she says. "We can go anywhere you like."

I can sense there is no squirming out of this, so I choose the Greek restaurant a few blocks away, because I always choose the Greek restaurant. I love it because it's called the White Tower even though it's in a one-story strip mall adorned with fake orange brick. I order my usual—the chicken lemon soup—and my mother cheats on my father and orders black coffee and fries.

"So have you heard from Kris lately?" she asks.

I tilt my water glass and fish out an ice cube with my fork, well aware that she has not brought me here to discuss my former cello teacher's battle with a mood disorder. "No."

She reaches across the table, and her sleeve ends up in a tiny puddle of water beneath my glass. "Okay, so then let's talk about you. You don't seem yourself, Faye. We're a little worried."

There is part of me that wants to bury my face in that generous Polish hand I know so well. How many times has it reached for me?

"Listen, Faye," she goes on, "you're at a difficult age. Lots of adopted kids have trouble in their teens."

Somehow, she thinks I will find it comforting that I'm a stereotype.

"Your dad and I were talking," she says. "Maybe we could plan another China trip. There's so much we didn't see last time. Things are still exploding over there, and I could probably even find some angle with the paper. I mean, pretty soon you may not even want to come with us anymore." She takes a sip of coffee and makes a face. "What do you think?"

I shrug, big and exaggerated, shoulders reaching for my ears.

She stares at me, forlorn. She covers inquiries into murdered children and violent rape cases without batting an eye. I am the only person who can make her look like this.

"I don't know," I say. "We were just there."

"Okay," she says. "It doesn't have to be Asia. You put so much pressure on yourself. Maybe you need a break from all the lessons and exams. Let's go somewhere, just the three of us. Cuba. Finland. Disneyland. You name it."

"Disneyland?" I repeat.

"Come on, Faye," she says. "What happened to my gypsy? People used to marvel at what a great traveler you were as a kid."

"Russia," I say.

It's her turn now. "Russia?"

I can't believe I said it, but I say it again, slowly this time. "Ru-sha."

The waitress comes with the food, and there's a brief reprieve. My mother's fries are too hot and she has to spit some out into a napkin. For my sake, she tries to be game. "The paper just sent Gerald to the western borderlands. They're not so much worried about nuclear fallout anymore as all the dirty fuels, like coal."

I don't mention that of the sixteen most polluted cities in the world, fourteen are in China. "I don't know. It's just an idea."

"Okay," she says. "Ideas are good. Your dad may be really into it. He's always wanted to see the Hermitage."

My phone rings. It's Celeste, so I let it go. "You can get that," my mother says.

After all these years, I've finally figured out that if you want Celeste's attention, you just have to ignore her. I guess if I were really nice, I'd sneak in and write that over a urinal in the guys' bathroom and save a lot of them a lot of time.

I shake my head. "It's just Celeste yanking my leash."

My mother begins downing her fries with the abandon of a naughty child wolfing candy. I try and remember how to do the Heimlich.

"Come on, Faye," she says with a full mouth. "We're worried because we love you."

After school the next day, the house is blissfully empty. Bev phones and I let it ring. Then I head upstairs and check my email.

Hello Little Bird. How are you? I am melancholy for quite a long time. I wish to be away from here. My life is not good. My future is not clear. Maybe I see you again some time, maybe no. I miss the snow. Can you believe? I trust you are well. Sincerely, Alexander Natieff (Sasha)

At first, I am flying with vindication. My Sasha is real. I did not imagine his big warm hands, his silly formality, his bright-blond belly hair. And then I crash with astonishing inevitability, a helpless sparrow going *smack-bang* into a spotless window.

Sasha is trapped in a place of screw-ups and heartache. He was the most interesting thing that ever happened to me, and now there's nothing I can do for him because this world is too big and too nasty.

There's a Chinese folk tale about true love that's popular with parents like mine who spend thousands of dollars and travel to the other side of the earth to create their families. According to the story, lovers are born with a magical thin red thread that connects them by their ankles, and no matter what they do or where they go, it's just a matter of time until they find each other.

"In those first days," my mother used to say, "you were so skinny, and with the bronchitis, you sounded like a seal. I was scared out of my wits. Then I noticed that every time you were upset or uncomfortable, you dug your tiny finger-nail into your thumb and made an okay sign. It was like you were telling me things were going to be okay, and I knew it was impossible to love anyone more than I loved you. It was like everything in our lives had led us to you, and you to us."

Sometimes we went to the farmers' market in St. Norbert, and afterward I'd lie in bed and imagine my birth mother carrying me around the stalls in her best willow basket. She would move quietly through the crowd, taking quick, sure steps with her petite feet until she found the perfect spot. She would set me down between my two favorite stalls—the one with free samples of rye bread and dill pickles and the one where they let me play with little Russian nesting dolls. As I gurgled, she would pull a red ribbon from her black hair and tie it to my ankle. Then my birth mother would flit away as quick as a hummingbird and my own mother would be there, twisting the other end of the ribbon around her wrist the way she fidgets with her watch when she's impatient. Then my mother would lift me in her arms, and I'd give her the okay sign and we'd go home.

I knew this was nothing more than a waking dream, but I didn't care—only the romance mattered. I let myself believe in the red thread for a long time, even after Bev told me that Santa wasn't real.

"My dad told me," she said. "He dresses up every year at the restaurant. He said it's just a good excuse for old guys to have girls sit on their laps."

"You can't see the real Santa," I said. "He's invisible. He comes when you're asleep."

"Your parents buy you the presents," she said. "I know. My mom keeps them downstairs, stacked behind the freezer."

But I didn't stop believing, even when I glimpsed the lies grown-ups tell themselves, like the time I did a little experiment over at Bev's place.

My mother, who is not naturally tidy—like most old-style journalists, her desk is a disaster of phone numbers on paper scraps, discarded story drafts and weeks-old newspapers—was forever wiping my face with her spit. It's like she lived in fear of someone thinking, *That child has dried milk on her face. She must have a bad mommy.*

So one time I was outside at Bev's. She was busy drawing little hearts on her pink skin with a stick while my mother sat on our front porch, editing a story. Now and then she would look up and wave, as if she couldn't care less that I was picking my nose the whole time. I was standing in the middle of the lawn, picking away, and she was fine with it, as if what happened at Bev's stayed at Bev's. As if it wasn't her concern.

Still I remained sweet, dutiful-by-nature Faye. I was studious and well-adjusted, with borderline OCD. I was best friends with perfect Celeste, descendent of the mighty Métis who mastered this frigid, mosquito-plagued flatland. My parents and I were three peas in a pod. I remained sweetly innocent for so long, like it was my due, when all the while I was being lied to by omission. I grew up with a "best of" propaganda reel of the Eastern Empire. It wasn't until I was old enough to look for myself that the fuller picture emerged.

I open the electronic file I had created before we left for China. Everything is ordered alphabetically. I scan a few entries, looking for some sign, something that ended the romance once and for all.

Re: Cultural Revolution

During the Cultural Revolution, music teachers were sometimes beaten to death by their own students for being "tainted artists." Many artists sent to the countryside for "re-education" resorted to cannibalism to survive.

Re: Demographic problems

Due to the selective abortion or abandonment of hundreds of thousands of girls over the course of China's one-child policy, the country is already suffering from a challenging shortfall of brides. By the middle of the century, it's estimated that surplus grooms will number in the millions. This sex-ratio gap has already led to a reported rise in the kidnapping and trafficking of marriageable women.

Re: Imperial culture

The Chinese traditionally conceive of heaven as but a mirror image of life on earth, a rigid hierarchical society administered by a giant bureaucracy in the sky.

Re: Suicide rates

Today, China is the only country in the world where more women kill themselves than men. Most use what's at hand, often agricultural chemicals.

Did it take nothing more than a few nights spent online, stockpiling historical notes and statistics, to snap me out of the dream? Or did I have to see it for myself, trudge through the suffocating humidity and hubris of the New China looking for a past that didn't exist?

By the time we got there, I knew the Chinese believed crickets to be lucky, but that they also thought it was fun to watch them fight to the death. I knew Chinese women had been treated like cattle since the empire began, knew individual human life had never held much value there. Confucius preached that family and duty came before all personal wishes. Duty to your family, to your godlike emperor, to your godlike state—so it's gone on through the centuries.

At least it was clear what my parents were hoping to find: a giddy trip down memory lane. My mother would rush to some god-awful, peach-colored hotel with a bootleg DVD stall out front. "There used to be a department store here where we got you that little knit jacket with the duck pockets. Little old ladies kept coming up and gesturing that you must be cold."

"It was twenty-one degrees," my father added, "and they were only happy if you were wrapped in wool."

Or my mother would make the taxi pull over. "There was a stall here where we went for noodles. We took a picture of you here, the one with a noodle hanging out of your mouth."

But I knew damn well this wasn't the whole story.

Re: TB and other orphanage illnesses
Common afflictions Westerners encountered while adopting baby girls from China: infected sores hidden beneath diapers, intestinal viruses and tuberculosis.

Re: True cautionary stories of international adoption
"The baby minder brought our frantically wailing one-year-old into the lobby so we could meet her for the first time. The baby was hysterical, crying so hard that the quarter-sized birthmark on her forehead was turning purple. I'm sure we look terrified, but nothing could prepare us for what came next. The minder suggested that she could take this one back and bring us another. Needless to say, we were horrified."

My parents loved to go on about how much the Chinese love children, and I saw it for myself. Wherever we went, families were happily out and about with their little ones, encouraging them to check out the foreigners, proudly pushing them forward to say, "hey-yo." So the million-dollar question is, how can they treat some children with such affection and others with such callousness?

When we tried to visit the orphanage where I spent my infancy, officials claimed it had been torn down and

Boston Public Library

Customer ID: * * * * * * * * * * *1541
Circulation system messages:
Patron status is ok.

Title: Your constant star
ID: 39999083127744
Due: 10/03/2014 23:59:59
Circulation system messages:
Item checkout ok.

Total items: 1
9/12/2014 3:46 PM
Checked out: 1
Overdue: 0
Hold requests: 0
Ready for pickup: 0

Circulation system messages:
End Patron Session is successful

Thank you for using the
3M SelfCheck™ System.

so took us to the deluxe model Emma and her family had gone back to renovate using church donations. They proudly showed us the rows of bright white cribs. Back at the original place, the one that is supposedly rubble now, they wrote little bios of us that were cherished like baby booties but probably mostly made up. *Chang is easily contented with her bottle and small rattle*, mine read. *She is very aware of her surroundings and likes music.*

My phone rings. It's Bev, so I let it go.

It rings again. Caller ID unavailable. When I pick up, there are street sounds—something big, like a bus or a truck. "Who is this?" I ask.

Nothing, then, "Why is Bev calling you?"

"Who *is* this?" I ask again.

"It doesn't matter," he says. "How do you know Bev?"

I hang up.

★ ★ ★

I dream of Dakota Forrester's *Sonatina for Cello and Piano I.* The bow takes on a life of its own, and the notes float in the clear mountain chill so sweetly and so sadly that it leaves Sasha and me breathless. All the weeping in the world is being distilled into those sweet, sad notes. They are the sound of pure sorrow, and so beautiful all you can do is let yourself surrender.

There's a knock—always a knock. "You'll be late for school, Faye," my mother says.

Downstairs, my father looks up from the paper and pokes me in the ribs. "You look like hell. Must be all that partying."

I know I must try and play along, but I'm still breathless from the mountain air. "Ha-ha," I manage before I'm saved by the buzz of my phone.

C came out this am. Dad walked out 15 min ago. Mom not talking. C looks like ghost. Keep u updated...Em/Liang

"So Faye says she's interested in Russia," my mother says. "Maybe we could do the Near East this fall."

"That was Emma," I say. "Colm came out this morning."

"Came out as in came out of the closet?" my mother asks.

"Yes," I say. "Came out as in he's gay."

My father smacks his paper in triumph. "I could've told you that years ago. Didn't I say that? That kid was always so meticulously groomed. No matter where we were, not a hair out of place."

My mother crosses her arms like an angry schoolteacher. "Christ, that poor kid. Lu and Billy will disown him."

I watch my father smugly congratulating himself, my mother passing judgment from her righteous perch, and suddenly I hate them both. Colm seemed like any other kid to me, but of course no one is as perceptive as those

74

two, no one as accepting. Sure, Lu and Billy have been back to China three times to donate money and build infrastructure for those who need it most, but who cares about such religious piffles?

"They actually seem to be working it out," I say. "Emma's relieved it's out there. She says God is mysterious."

My father looks slightly deflated. "Yeah? Well, there's hope for all of us if ol' Lu and Bill are loosening up in their old age."

"Emma's not always the most reliable source," my mother says. "She can talk herself into anything."

I pour myself some orange juice and try not to puke up the pulp. "I'm just telling you what she said."

"Poor Colm," she says again, as if she's given him a second thought in years.

★ ★ ★

The next day, Celeste and my mother ambush me after school. Though Carson's days are numbered, he's there too, grinning his million-dollar smile like I've just been pranked on TV. He's the kind of guy who's used to things coming easily, but when his heart breaks, that easy grin will never be the same.

Before I know it, Carson is gone and Celeste and my mother are on either side of me, close enough to bump my bony hips, and we're moving along the sidewalk as if in a six-legged race. After a stretch of days well above freezing, mild enough to flood basements, a cold front has moved in. In April, after the melt, no one has the heart to go back to full winter gear, and I'm almost grateful for the body warmth.

My mother stubs her toe on a crack in the cement and pretends it didn't hurt. "We're going to the coffee shop," she says.

"Why?" I ask.

"So you can't hide in your room," Celeste says. She's rubbing against me in a way that would make many a high-school boy very happy.

"Do I have a choice?" I ask.

"No," Celeste says.

It's crowded, so we end up in the corner near the bathroom. Celeste orders a hot chocolate, hold the whipped cream. I stick with ice water, in protest. My mother sets her towering cup of brewed black coffee in the middle of the table and reaches into her sensible faux-leather reporter's briefcase. She pulls out a piece of paper and clasps it in her hand as if it's some top-secret message. Celeste warms her fingers on her mug and avoids eye contact.

"Faye, hon," my mother says, "we're here because we need you to talk to us."

I take a sip of water. My mother is not one for endearments like "sweetie" or "honey."

"O-kay," I say slowly.

"We love you," she says. "And we're worried. You're not yourself. We need you to talk to us so we can help."

She places the ultrasound of the Little Alien on the table. "Tina found this on your closet floor yesterday when she was vacuuming."

It takes me a moment to process this—Tina is the housekeeper. I stupidly didn't put the Little Alien back where it belongs, hidden in the pristine box, and Tina with the buckteeth and thick Spanish accent found it and then gave it to my mother.

Celeste continues to treat her beverage like a mini hand-warmer. "What gives?" she asks. "What's going on with you?"

"What do you want me to say?" I ask.

My mother's eyes are turning hamster pink. I try and remember the last time she cried—probably not since last year, when she saw the rows upon rows of metal cribs at Emma's jazzed-up orphanage. "I don't know, Faye. You tell us. Just talk to us." She pushes the sonogram across the table to me, just like Bev did. *Why does everyone keep doing that?* I want to ask. *I don't even want it.*

"We need to talk about this, Faye," she says.

I don't want her to cry here, outside the toilet-paper-less bathroom of a crowded coffee shop, but it's too late. "What's the big deal?" I ask. "I found it. It was in a recycling bin at the library. I'd printed some stuff off that I didn't need and when I went to recycle it, there it was. It kind of weirded me out. Who would throw that away?"

My mother flips the image over. "It's been written on."

"I know," I say. "Somebody wrote on it."

Celeste picks it up and studies it like her eyesight isn't perfect 20/20. "Isn't this your printing?"

It strikes me that Celeste is here because my mother needs her. Because the big no-nonsense reporter who holds her own with the boys can't handle this on her own. She's only tough when the drama doesn't involve *her*.

"No," I say, "it's not. I told you. I found it. Somebody else wrote on it."

It dawns on me that they think I might be pregnant, that "my problem" might be something as obvious as that. "I can assure you, it's not mine. Unless you believe in the virgin birth."

My mother presses her lips together, which at least gives them a little color. "Please understand, hon. We're not accusing you of anything. We just want to know what's going on. We want to be here for you."

Part of me wants to crawl into her wide Polish lap and let her tell me stories about her blue-collar childhood. About the boys playing cowboys and Indians who tied the littlest one up and made him eat a rotten tomato.

About her brother fishing a bike out of the creek and fixing it up to look like new. About how she cried and cried because her Sleepy Head rag doll never opened her eyes and so her baba had to draw eyeballs over the lids.

"I know," I say. "I know that. I just need a little space these days."

Celeste fishes an ice cube out of my glass and pops it into her mouth. She does these kinds of things because she and her sister share everything, but I want to choke her until it pops back out.

"Okay, but since when do you want to go to Russia?" she asks.

Her words are garbled because of the ice. I pull my glass toward me, so close I'm almost cuddling it. "Excuse me?"

"Your mom says you're talking about going to Russia."

Of all the little secrets I'm keeping, the thought of my best friend finding out about Sasha makes me the craziest. How crazy is that? "So?" I say. "What do you care? There's lots of places I want to go."

Celeste puts both elbows on the table, as if readying herself for an arm wrestle. "Okay, but the thing is, Faye, you've been kind of a bitch, and that's not like you. You're just being so weird."

I sit across a wobbly table from these two people I both love and hate, and I don't know what to tell them.

I cannot explain myself, as if telling enough little lies can spin a web large enough to hold you in its grasp, dumb and unreachable.

All I know for certain is that I will do as Bev Novak has asked, because she and I have unfinished business and, as a tried-and-true OCD freak, I must see it through to the end.

And as specks of hard April snow begin to bounce off the window, all I can think about is that it would be real spring in Southern China right now, which is good, considering some dirt-poor field hand or dirt-poor field hand turned exploited factory worker is probably abandoning a baby girl outside a train station or beside a stall of muddy yams.

Even if it's warm out, the baby will be dressed in many layers, and if she is not wailing for her life yet, she will be very soon.

PART TWO

Bev.

FIVE

I get to the coffee shop ten minutes early, because to get what you want, it's a little about luck and a lot about positioning. You have to be in the right place at the right time to seize the day.

I sit on one of the velvety purple couches that Lara would've flipped over during her *color soothes the soul* phase. I pick the far corner, so Faye will know this is serious—no running out so easily. When she called yesterday, she sounded a little unsure. She said the housekeeper found the ultrasound of the Little Alien and asked if it was Faye's, which totally cracked me up, even though Faye most definitely was not laughing. But we're down to the nitty-gritty now. She is either into this or she isn't.

The place is full, and the girl behind the counter, who looks like she's auditioning for the role of "fat Goth chick," glares at me now and then. At one point, I say loudly, "I'm waiting for someone," but this doesn't make a difference because that's the thing with people these days—they have no respect. On the bus, it's not the girls who get up for you when they see you're pregnant, it's the guys. Which is why I fricking hate the bus. Some people have respect, and some are lazy bastards, and you never know which one is going to be mouth-breathing beside you.

Maybe I should've told Denise the social worker that was my number-one criteria: anybody raising my kid has to teach them respect. Only I know what she would've said. She would've looked at me with that oh-so-patient, acne-scarred face of hers and said, *Okay, respect. What do you mean by that, Bev? Maybe you could elaborate.* And I would've said something like *Respect, Denise. R-E-S-P-E-C-T. Do you need to look it up?*

When I was a kid, Ray used to call me his "chubby little diva," which he thought was very funny, but these days, it seems about right, since I'm getting rounder by the minute and almost everything pisses me off. Like how from the minute we met, Denise rubbed me the wrong way.

"You can't just place an ad," she said. "There's a process. If you trust me, we can do this in a way that works for everyone."

It's like she thought I was retarded, and I almost lost it. "You thought I was serious? I just wrote that to lighten things up a bit. I'm not stupid. Don't talk to me like I'm stupid."

Then she backpedaled like crazy, told me how she'd been a teen mother too, that she'd made a lot of mistakes and only got her social-work degree after attending the school of hard knocks, blah, blah, blah. *All that effort,* I wanted to say, *and still a beauty-school dye job. How much do they pay you down at Family Services?*

A red jacket flashes by the window, and I know it's Mannie. I can tell by the way the jacket's flapping in the wind, trailing after him like a cape. I swear he leaves it unzipped so I will give him shit and tell him to do it up because "it's cold, moron."

I slouch down a little, even though it's pointless. It won't keep him from finding me, and it'll only shift the stabbing pain from my lower back to my right butt cheek.

"He seems to be standing tall as a little soldier right on your sciatic nerve," the doctor had said when I last saw him. "Maybe with a little massage, he'll shift on around." There was something about the way he said it, Mr. Casual and Collected, that made me want to scratch his face off. *It seems you've lost an arm,* he could've been saying. *Here, have this tissue—maybe it'll stop the bleeding.*

The little bell above the door tinkles, and Mannie looks around like some cowboy entering a saloon. When he sees me, he puts on his Mr. Tough Guy look, his lips set into a little pout, his eyes small. The closer he gets, the smaller the eyes get and the bigger the pout, but I try not to laugh, because it would only get him worked up.

"What, did you follow me here?" I ask.

He stands over me, feet apart, arms crossed. His nose is running, and he's wearing too much body spray. "What was I supposed to do?"

I lean forward, and my tailbone feels like I just sat on a cactus. I want to sucker punch Mannie in the balls, but I know that will ruin everything. I remain Ms. Casual and Collected. "You could stop following me around."

"You don't tell me nothing," he says. "What am I supposed to do?"

I lean back and gasp as a porcupine slides down my right leg.

"It still hurts?" he asks.

"Yes," I say. "It still hurts. And it's not 'nothing.' It's 'anything.' 'You don't tell me anything.'"

Mannie starts to rock back and forth, like he always does when I correct him—it's like his weird-ass version of a nod.

"Whatever," he says. "Don't change the subject, Bev. What do you want me to do?"

It reminds me of when Ray first found out Mannie and I were together. I'd only been back in Winnipeg a few months, but I could already tell that Ray and me in his tiny condo was not going to work. When he'd sat me down, I thought he was going to tell me I had to go back to Lara in Vancouver.

"What's this I hear about you and the kid in the kitchen?"

He'd been trying to quit smoking and was going through a lot of gum. He chewed with his mouth open, like he meant business.

"What do you want me to do?" I asked. "Sit here by myself knitting you socks? How am I supposed to meet people?"

"I don't know," he said. "Go to the gym, go to school. You're the one who wanted to do the correspondence thing. Shouldn't kids your age be with other kids your age?"

"You hired him," I said, "and he *is* my age."

He opened a new piece of gum and spat the old one into the wrapper. I was pretty sure he was putting on this concerned-dad charade for some new woman in the picture, and I was right.

"Don't change the subject," he said. "This is about you. You got to keep your eye on the ball. You're not a baby anymore."

You got that right, I should've said. *All your babies are grown up, and we've all seen the concerned-dad act.*

Mannie keeps rocking now, and the waft of his body spray starts to make me feel queasy. I lean forward even though it hurts like a bitch and grab his shoulder. "Stop that or I might hurl."

He wedges himself in beside me, puts his arm around my shoulder and squeezes softly, like we're at the hospital and someone just died. "You still feeling sick? I thought that was getting better."

I drag myself out from under him. If having the Little Alien hurts worse than what I'm feeling right now, then I will die on the delivery table and Ray will no longer have to worry about whether I've got my eye on the ball.

The bell over the door tinkles again, and I know without looking that it must be Faye. Now and then, for no reason, I can tell what's going to happen—sort of a second sight. Like, even when I was ten, I knew Lara would not get over Ray anytime soon, even though she pretended every minute of every day that she was. And last year, I knew Ray was seeing health-nut Charlotte even though he never told me about her until he decided not to invest in her kickboxing studio.

But having a little second sight doesn't mean you can just sit back and relax—far from it. I have to suck up the jabs and think fast, because Mannie is here, his dumb, tough face turned all sucky and concerned, and there's nothing I can do. There's no time to get rid of him.

He inches over. "Bev?"

Faye spots us and it's all I can do not to shove him away. "Yeah. Yes. I just need to breathe here without any stink, okay? I just need a little space to breathe."

When I look up, Faye is standing a few feet away, staring at us with her cool, black eyes. She's wearing a brown hoodie with extra-long sleeves, but I can see she's picking at her fingers. I remember her doing that whenever she got nervous. I'd say something wild like "Let's write messages with our own blood," and Faye would *pick, pick, pick.* Or Ray would tell me to tell Lara to either put on some lipstick or go back to bed, and Faye would *pick, pick, pick.*

Mannie doesn't budge. "Can I help you?"

Part of me wants to slam my fist into his thigh, give him the ten-minute charley horse that one of my half brothers taught me. But part of me wants to laugh, because Mannie the Hero is almost as ridiculous as Mannie the Cowboy.

"This is Faye," I say. "My friend."

Mannie gets up and the shift in the couch almost makes me howl bloody murder. He leans across the coffee table as far as he can without falling over and offers his hand. "Mannie here. Any friend of Bev's is a friend of mine."

Faye stops fidgeting to shake politely. Fat Goth Girl comes up behind her with a dingy wet cloth covered in flu virus. "You guys going to order anything?"

Mannie looks down at me, and I look up at Faye.

"I have a card," she says. "What do you want?"

Fat Goth turns away as if we're not worth her time. *You dress like a vampire,* I want to say, *but I bet you go home to your mommy every night. She's probably a real-estate agent, and you borrow her silver sedan to get to your shitty, pocket-change little gig.*

"I don't do hot drinks," Mannie says. "I need something cold, with a kick to it."

Faye starts to pick again. It's hard enough to think these days without Mannie being so Mannie. I tell myself to focus. My game legs may be wobbly, but they haven't given out yet. "No, this time it's on me," I say.

Faye pulls the card out of her pocket. "No, really. I've still got lots left on this. What do you want?"

Mannie pushes past my knees and scoots around the coffee table to Faye. He does it in three swift steps, quick as a cat, before I can stop him. Even wearing a filthy apron and hairnet in Ray's kitchen, there was something catlike about him—sleek black hair, dark-green eyes, arms so lean you could see every muscle.

"I got to look at what they have," he says, then turns back to me. "You want juice? Juice would be good."

Since he found out I'm pregnant, Mannie has turned into a fricking dietitian, which is a laugh and a half coming from a guy who lives on instant noodles and weed and still looks cut. When he bugs me about taking my prenatal vitamin, I want to take the pink bullet-shaped pill and shove it up his nostril.

"Don't tell me what's good for me," I say.

Though he's known her for all of one minute, Mannie turns to Faye for backup. "I'm just saying."

Faye nods politely but looks ready to bolt.

"Whatever," I say. "Juice is fine. Anything but apple."

They go to the counter, and Fat Goth takes a very long time getting three bottles out of a fridge. Mannie says something to Faye, who keeps nodding politely.

For the fourth time today, the Little Alien has the hiccups. They're steady as a heartbeat, and the first time I noticed them, maybe two weeks ago, that's exactly what I thought I was hearing. When the little tapping stopped after a few minutes, I wondered if that was it, if the Little Alien was gone and now Mannie would shut up and Lara would start crying over something else and Ray would forgive his chubby little diva for not killing the Little Alien earlier and I would have some peace.

Mannie holds out a poppy-seed bagel on a paper plate.

"What's that?" I ask.

He puts it on the table and settles in beside me. "What does it look like?"

Faye sits down in the overstuffed armchair across from us and opens a bottle of iced tea. She plays with the cap, like she doesn't want to interfere.

"Thanks for coming," I say to her. I can sense Mannie getting ready to pout, and I know I don't have much time. "You remember your old baba made that poppy-seed cake and your dad walked around with little black bits in his teeth all afternoon?"

Faye smiles a little and keeps playing with her cap.

Mannie drains his energy drink as quickly and loudly as he can, then slams the can on the coffee table like he's just done something great. "So you guys go way back?"

Most women find Mannie pretty easy on the eyes, but there is no way he is Faye's type. She looks at him like she's thinking about something else, like somebody just gave her a math problem she can't figure out. And she can't quite believe she can't figure it out 'cause she's really good at math.

I take a chance, because sometimes you have to go with your gut, you just have to rip that Band-Aid off. "She's going to help me with the interview."

"You getting another job?" Mannie asks. "I thought we'd been through this."

This is moronic even for Mannie. Since he found out he was going to be a daddy, he's become not just a nutrition expert, but Mr. Do-The-Right-Thing. He quit dealing to make two-for-one pizzas all night. He acted glad when I quit waitressing at the pancake place because it was "too hard on me." Whenever I ask how the hell we're going to pay for food, he says, "Don't worry, babe. Sit down. Screw Ray. We're good—we're together. Don't worry."

I want to grab his tongue and twist. But Faye is *pick, pick, picking,* and I must remain casual and collected, Ms. Relaxed and Controlled. I remember that when actors are sitting around a table on TV, they often eat something to appear natural, so I take a bite of bagel. The poppy seeds stick to the roof of my mouth like sand.

"The adoption interview," I say.

Mannie crosses his arms and slouches back in the couch like he might take a nap. "Just like that, eh? You decide. You decide everything. You know best, Bev. You know goddamn best."

If he were more of a man, he would've got up and walked out. He would've at least had the dignity to know when he wasn't wanted. But no, Mannie doesn't quit a job, he just complains about the crap pay. He drives such a shit truck that it can't make it through three nights of deliveries. He'd rather sulk about how I'm treating him than face the fact that I'd rather serve pancakes to seniors in matching windbreakers and their mouth-breathing grandchildren for the rest of my life than raise a kid with him. I'd rather have a girls' night out with Denise the social worker. I'd rather pop the zits on Ray's back, like my poor, victimized mother used to.

But that's the difference between Mannie and me. He's had a shitty life, so it's like he doesn't know any better, whereas I know I was not meant to fetch packets of rock-hard butter that people will try to spread only to end up mutilating their toast. I was meant to run the restaurant. Ray may be a prick, but he taught me this: sometimes you're going to be short of cash, but you've always got to have a plan.

"You're giving the baby up?" Faye asks.

I swish some juice around in my mouth and nod. The Little Alien is hiccupping again, as if it knows we're talking about it.

"Why her?" Mannie asks. "What does she have to do with this?"

Because I want to show Ray how it's done. Because I don't know anyone else who's adopted. Because even after I moved back to this third-rate burb, I barely thought of Faye at all, not until after I got into this shit, when I knew I needed a plan, and then I couldn't get her out of my head.

"Because," I say, "we go way back."

I wait for Mannie to bring up Betty, his sainted pseudo-mother, wait for the sad-sack story about how he knows a thing or two about this stuff and maybe he should have a say because it's his kid. But he shuts up and keeps pouting.

Faye is looking at my bump, and I think of the time Lara told Faye that she had wise eyes. It was right after Lara's hysterectomy, when she lay milking it on the couch for days, hopped up on OxyContin. "You look like you got judgment," she told Faye, and we beelined it out of there, away from the stench of Calming Cucumber body lotion and greasy hair and flat ginger ale.

The Little Alien goes quiet, like it can feel Faye's eyes on my stomach. For the last five minutes, it hasn't jabbed or moved, has left me in peace for once, as if it knows its fricking future is at stake here.

No one has to say a word, and I can sense it's a done deal. You have to be prepared for a few curveballs. You have to trust your instincts and get a little lucky.

"When's the interview?" Faye asks.

"Three days," I say. "Tuesday. Four fifteen. I'll be exactly thirty-one weeks."

Denise and I pick Faye up outside her school on Tuesday as requested. I can tell by the way she's standing, hands shoved in pockets and skinny legs stiff as Popsicle sticks, that she's been waiting for a while. It's sunny, and she has to walk through a little pile of slush to get to the curb.

Denise lets her in the back of the minivan and slides the door closed so hard, you'd think she was a jail guard.

I look back and give Faye a little wave. She smiles like she doesn't really mean it, and her dainty Chinese nose crinkles a little. *I know*, I want to say. *It stinks like rancid chocolate milk and the smokes Denise must sneak when her kids aren't around.*

"It's close," Denise says. "Maybe ten minutes away."

Now and then, the craziness of things hits you right between the eyes and you have to suck it up. You can't let yourself think about the fact that you're suddenly in a social worker's nasty beater with someone you never thought you'd see again, going to meet some barren couple named Olef and Helga who happen to live in the old neighborhood.

You have to suck it up, let the current take you over the waves, into the spray, onto the rocks. The ocean was the only thing I liked about living out west. I hated the drizzle. I hated the do-gooder two-faced bitches who talked about saving the trees while they stole your boyfriend. But the ocean was all right. Everything going with the flow—don't even try to paddle, just wait and see where things will wash up.

"What the hell were you thinking?" Ray had asked. "That kid is too stupid to bus tables, never mind raise a kid.

And you—you think you're ready? Lara was always *go easy on her, Ray,* always *don't be such a hardass.* But look what it gets you. What's your plan?"

"Don't lecture me," I said. "I'm not going to make having kids and getting divorced my new hobby. I'm not keeping it."

"You're not keeping it," he said. "Right, I can see that. You've obviously looked after things and have just been eating too many Long Johns."

The Long Johns remark was a low fricking blow. Sometimes, when we still lived in Winnipeg and Lara stayed in bed late on the weekends, Ray would take me to the bakery up the street, and Long Johns were my favorite treat. He teased me about my "Long John gut," but we still kept going, and in between cell-phone calls, he'd talk about his problems with beverage deliveries and leaky roofs and short-order chefs who stole, like I wasn't just a kid. And so the blow was all the lower because he was right. I hadn't looked after things, had let week after week go by without booking an appointment at the clinic. But I hadn't wanted to think about any of it, not the nauseating tightness in my gut, not the little hand vac they'd stick between my legs, because sometimes thinking too much gets you nowhere.

Look at Lara. She's gone from thinking she's fat because her mommy died when she was five to thinking she's fat because she's an emotional eater or because Ray is a sociopath. She has a bad back because her fillings are made of mercury, or because her chair at work is toxic, or because Ray is a sociopath. She hashes things over and over, endlessly gazing at her stretch-marked navel and tying her panties up in knots.

Maybe that's why I always end up back with Mannie, why I find it so hard to stay mad at him. He never seems to worry about what happened five minutes ago, never mind five years. Except when it comes to his foster mom, the sainted Betty, but he only really talks about her in the morning, if we stay in bed for a bit and he lights a joint. I can tell when he's going to start, because he rolls over to me and brushes my hair out of my face like they do in the movies and smiles, his face still puffy and soft like a little kid's. Once I knew the signs, though, I could get up to pee before the Bettyfest even began.

Mannie has no postsecondary, no real smarts, but he is a man of action. When I met him, he'd already been charged with strike number two and his probation officer was on speed dial. Mannie had sworn to him that he was done with joyriding, was seeing a new girl, "the fricking heiress of a restaurant chain," but there were times when he'd show up at Ray's condo door and hold out a set of keys like a bouquet.

Pretty much everybody in my family has their addiction. With Lara, it's food and navel-gazing. With Ray, it's money and wives. With Jill, it was some married record producer with buckteeth. All of my half sibs have their own "thing," except for the oldest, the twins Karla and Kim, who don't stay in touch, so I don't know. For years, I kept waiting to see what my poison would be. I'd seen enough boozers and junkies at my "alternative" West Coast schools to know what a fricking bore they were. There was no way I was going there. Then I met Mannie and, lo and behold, found out I couldn't get enough of speeding through suburbs in stolen suvs. It's dangerous, it's pointless, but when you're there, unbuckled, nothing applies to you. Nothing. You run the red, you fling a kid's car seat out the window, it doesn't matter if you live or die. Afterward, the high sticks around for a while, the thought-less, breathless rush, and when Mannie touches you, he is a hungry cat, not a two-bit dealer who says *nothing* instead of *anything*, and you let yourself be devoured.

Still, I hated Ray that day he dared to get so pissed at me, because he was right. I'd screwed up. I didn't need some hypocrite to tell me that, and I knew even before he said it how it was going to end, because even when we're royally pissed, Ray and I understand each other.

"I can't support this," he'd said. "It wouldn't be right. The gravy train ends today. Let Big Daddy Carjacker support you."

Giving it up for adoption never would've occurred to him. You don't give away something that's rightfully yours. Better kill the thing than give it to a stranger, much less a stranger who lives south of the tracks, where the odd tract of public housing brings everything else down.

In the old neighborhood, the farther you get from the river, the less posh it becomes. Within a few minutes, the big old trees and big old houses with dormers and trellises turn into rows of stucco-covered boxes with tacky trimmed hedges. Ray and Lara don't agree on much, but whenever they ventured a mile or two south of our old place on Montrose, they said the houses "lost all pedigree." *Pedigree* is a word they started to use a lot when they got the bright idea to get a basset hound to breed when money was a little tight one winter.

"Oh, the stench," Lara always says when she tells the story. "Who could have anticipated the profound stench? My eyes water just thinking about that animal."

"Watch for Taylor," Denise says. "It's a right on Taylor."

Suddenly, I hate Denise almost as much as I hate Ray. The afternoon sun is so bright in Denise's beater that it hurts, and I wonder how old she must be. Forty?

Her makeup has sunk into the little lines around her eyes, and in this light, there are signs of a faint mustache above her lip. She's probably at that age when most people start needing glasses, although she tries to dress younger. *If you got some glasses*, I want to say, *maybe you'd notice the 'stache and stop squinting in that really unattractive way whenever we're going through forms.*

"Up there," Faye says. "Taylor."

We stop in front of a bungalow much like the kind Lara rented when we first moved to Vancouver—beige stucco, concrete steps, two square windows staring at you on either side of the front door.

"Here we are," says Denise, like we're her kids and we've just arrived at an amusement park. I hate the way Denise is always too much of something—too down-to-business, too touchy-feely, too I've-been-in-your-shoes, too cheery, like she's trying to live down the fact that she's got a homemade tattoo that says *Billy* above her left wrist. When I asked her about it, she said it was from a long time ago, in another life, and it reminds her every day how far she's come. Which seemed like a load of shit to me, and I wasn't in the mood to let her get away with it. "Right," I said, "and I bet it would hurt like a bugger and cost a lot to have it removed."

The front sidewalk has been completely cleared of all signs of slush. The concrete isn't even wet, as if someone has not only shoveled but also blow-dried the thing. Before we're even halfway up the walk Helga opens the door and ushers us in.

The living room looks smaller than the one in our house in Vancouver, but it's hard to tell because there's a lot more furniture. After Ray dumped her, Lara went all minimalist, but these people have obviously gone to town at some big-box store—matching couch and love seat, matching end tables, matching recliners. The sofa-size painting of lily pads must've been part of the deal.

Helga takes our coats one by one and piles them in the crook of her arm. "Sit, sit," she says, pointing from one seat to another. "Make yourself at home. Olef's just making coffee, but we have tea, soda. What would you like?"

She heads to the hall closet before we can answer. She is somewhere between sturdy and chubby, maybe thirty pounds overweight, which is about what I expected. In her file, she listed baking and Aquasize as two of her main hobbies.

Denise takes a seat primly on the love seat. The purple of her sweater isn't a bad color for her, but it's starting to ball and makes her breasts look saggy. The sleeves are just long enough to cover her wrists and the tattoo.

I sit in one of the hideous recliners, and Helga comes up behind Faye and leads her to the other one. "Now, what can I get you guys?"

I glance over at Faye, who has said all of four words since we picked her up. "Do you have any diet grapefruit?" I say.

"Oh," Helga says. "No. But we have diet everything else. You name it."

There's something about her that reminds me of Heather, Ray's daughter with his second wife, Val. They both look like they could be the milkmaid on a package of butter—rosy cheeks, big teeth and bigger thighs.

"Surprise me," I say.

Helga blinks nervously, like I've just told her that if she guesses my weight correctly, the baby is hers. "Righto. A surprise it is."

"Coffee would be lovely," Denise says.

Faye gives a little wave with her tiny hand. "I'm good."

Olef appears with a plate of banana bread. The file said he owns a sports memorabilia store, and he looks exactly like the kind of guy who watches—but doesn't play—a lot of sports. His face is shiny and pale, and if it weren't for the just-baked banana bread, you could probably smell his sweaty golf shirt.

Denise repeats the introductions with Olef as he passes out cake with no napkins. He looks eager and nervous, that nice guy who only checks you out when he thinks you're not looking. Except the vibe I'm getting is anything but horniness. He wouldn't notice if I had a unibrow and one leg; all I am to him is a walking womb—a non-junkie, healthy, blond womb.

He wrote in the file that he's wanted to be a dad for as long as he can remember. His own father had been a Wolf Cub leader and a hockey coach and played Santa at the community club children's party. Olef also wrote that Helga is the "light of his life" and that he married her even though she'd had a hysterectomy at twenty-four.

Helga comes back with the coffee and a no-name diet cola. Denise takes her coffee black, and somehow I know that both Helga and Olef will take the works: half-and-half and two sugar cubes each. They settle down on the couch together like two peas in a faux-suede pod.

"Well, it's so great to finally meet you, Bev," Helga says.

It hits me that I know all I need to know about these people. Thanks to their profile folder, I know more about them than I do about my own family. Helga is an executive assistant at a big insurance firm, which means she's a glorified secretary, but will quit when a baby arrives. Her mother died from uterine cancer when Helga was eight, so she wants to be there for every moment of her children's lives. The biggest challenge in their marriage is that he's a saver and she's a shopper. Their favorite place in the world is their cabin at Matlock Beach. They are both Lutheran and, though they don't attend church, will probably christen their children "because they both found a great sense of security growing up within a community of faith." They will "welcome this baby into their lives with much joy and be fully prepared to maintain ongoing contact with his/her birth family."

Denise picks the crumbs off her pants one by one. Faye squeezes her thighs together like she's horny. Olef and Helga sit and wait, trying not to stare at the bump. What kind of guy wants to have kids more than anything else in the world and marries someone with a bum uterus? Apparently this one, with the homemade banana bread and shiny, desperate face.

"Bev has had a chance to get familiar with your file," Denise says. "I know she has some questions for you."

The straw in my drink is the bendy kind they give you in hospitals. I take a long swig, and the Little Alien jabs my pelvic bone. "Helga, you want to be a stay-home mom. Olef, you run a store that's been open for just over a year. What if the business fails? Do you have a plan?"

They are surprised, but hungry, and recover quickly. Olef tells me he's worked in retail for years, and if his own place fails, stores are always looking for good people, good managers.

After that, we roll along nicely. The Little Alien jabs, pointless questions pop into my head, and Helga and Olef answer dutifully. Would they both be hands-on parents? *Yes.* Would the baby have cousins close in age? *Yes, a girl and a boy in Calgary, ages two and four, a boy in Brandon, eighteen months, and three girls in Winnipeg, twelve, eight and five.* Are there good schools in the area? *Yes, an elementary two blocks away, a bus to the high school.* Do you have a nursery ready?

Yes. A blinding-yellow box of a room with nothing but a glider rocking chair, probably from the big-box store. We all crowd into the doorway except for Helga, who walks right into the middle and holds out her arms like she's about to sing opera.

"We both automatically thought yellow," she says. Her chipper voice echoes against the bare walls, and her cheeks are suddenly more blotchy than rosy.

"It's like sunflowers," Faye says.

Helga hugs herself and giggles, as if Faye has just uncovered some in-joke between her and Olef. "Isn't that funny. The paint's called *Sunflower Fields.*"

Good ol' Faye rescues the milkmaid from blotchiness and tears. I knew there was a reason I brought her along.

I give Denise a let's-wrap-this-up raise of the eyebrows. "Well," I say, "you have a lovely home. This has been great. It was so nice meeting you in person."

"Us too," Olef says. He takes my hand awkwardly, grasps it in both of his like I've just won an award. His hands aren't sweaty like I expected. They're smooth and warm and firm.

Denise pulls them both aside into the kitchen, and the grown-ups chatter quietly amongst themselves for a minute. When we get to the van, Faye and I both get in back, as if Denise is just our driver.

"They were nice," Faye says.

"Yeah," I say. "They were nice. But I'm not sure they're the ones."

Denise turns on the ignition and busies herself pretending to adjust the mirror.

Faye starts *pick, pick, picking.* "I don't know if I can do this," she says.

"What?" I ask. "Can't do what?"

"This," she says. "This whole thing."

"I know it's weird," I say. "But I need some backup, Faye. You know Lara, she used to say you had good judgment. You were just a kid and she thought you were the Queen of Good Judgment."

Denise peers at us through the rearview mirror. She looks tired, like she might be coming down with something. "Well, Bev, you've chosen a few files for consideration. We can meet with those couples as well, if you like. You're in your third trimester now, Bev, and we'll want to move things along, but we want you to feel totally comfortable with your decision."

Faye stares down at her poor, picked-over fingers.

"It has the hiccups," I say. "Do you want to feel? It's bizarre."

I grab Faye's hand and hold it against the bump.

"That's hiccups?" she asks.

I nod and hold her hand there until we're practically back at the school.

"You sure you don't want us to take you home?" Denise asks.

Faye is already out the door. "This is great. I have a late cello practice in the band room."

It warms my heart to think even perfect Faye is a liar.

SIX

For the first time, I dream about Faye. It's like I'm a fly on the wall as she and Mannie sit down to dinner with her parents. They're eating something pink, maybe baked salmon, and I can tell Mannie hates it. They keep asking him polite questions like "Do you have brothers and sisters?" and "What part of town did you grow up in?", but he's mumbling and I can't hear his answers. Faye smiles happily as he mumbles, like she finds the whole thing amusing.

"What the hell are you doing?" I say to him. "How do you even know them?"

But he can't hear me, of course, and when the Little Alien wakes me up, I have to pee really bad. I kick Mannie as I struggle to get up, like it's his fault he was in my dream.

I swear, it's as if those days when I was a kid on Montrose barely existed after I left. Then I went back, to the big bare trees and snow-rutted back lanes, and I saw Faye and I started remembering all kinds of things about River Heights, when Ray was still pretending that the restaurants weren't in the crapper and Lara still thought there was something she could do to make him want her again. Back when my Big Sis Jill still came to stay and made hilariously sad faces behind Lara's back.

Maybe that's all what Denise calls "baby brain"—most of your mind gets fuzzier than morning tongue, but some things get super clear.

I sit on the toilet for several minutes, but all I manage is a good burp. Denise and Dr. Kohut keep saying that if I'm getting constipated, I have to get lots of fiber in my diet, which makes me want to puke chewed-up bran all over their precious files. I know I need to eat broccoli or dried fruit or fricking wood chips, but the Little Alien wants starches. It likes to play with knives inside of me, and it likes to carb out on noodles, processed cheese and white bread. Lara would turn over in her tanning bed if she knew the way I was eating these days.

"I feel like I should be there," she said last week over the phone. "I'm going to book a flight."

"We're fine," I said. "Please don't."

"Why won't you let me come?" she asked. "Why don't you ever let me in? You're my little girl. Are you eating good? Is he being good to you? What's his name, Danny—is he being good to you?"

"He's good," I said. "We're good."

"What about Ray? Is he being a shit about this? You know he made me get an abortion once. Eighteen months after you were born. Did I ever tell you that? He said six was enough, like he was talking about pairs of shoes. Sometimes I lose track of what I've shared with you. I wanted to protect you, baby. I've always wanted to protect you."

"Yeah, I know," I said. "You told me. But he's fine. I can take care of Ray."

"That's my strong Bev," she said. "I love how strong you are. But don't forget about your mama. I want to help. I want to be there for you."

"I know," I said. "I'll keep you updated."

She'd sighed then. "Oh, my baby Bev…"

"You okay in there?" Mannie shouts though the bathroom door.

The Little Alien shifts around and delivers a swift punch below my ribs. Dr. Kohut says the fetus can recognize voices already, and I wonder if the Little Alien is already as irritated by Mannie's verbal diarrhea as I am.

There's a knock on the door. "Bev, you okay?"

Yes, I should've said to Lara. *He's being so good to me I want to kill him.*

The Little Alien delivers a double kick to the groin, and pain slashes down my right leg. "Yes. I'm okay, moron."

After the first trimester, when I didn't feel ready to hurl every minute and my gut busted open the zipper of my best jeans, I moved in with Mannie, and things were bearable for a while. He worked nights at the pizza place, and if the place was a sty, at least I had most of it to myself. Mannie's roommate, Warren, a big fat gangbanger who fancied himself some kind of street warrior, slept all day and went out at night, dealing with shit way out of Mannie's league. But Warren was actually a bit of a neat freak, always telling Mannie to get his shit out of the sink. And he never brought girls back unless it was for business. I figured maybe he was a closet case trying hard to cover up with a macho criminal act.

"What's with him?" I asked once. "He doesn't even look at me."

Mannie stuck his tongue in my ear and purred. "He blames you for turning me into a pussy."

I laughed and let his tongue twirl around. "You did that all yourself."

I laughed harder than I had in a long time, because it was true. When I first met Mannie, he seemed so unpredictable, skinny and muscular at the same time, always watching me with those green cat eyes. He carried stacks of dirty dishes like he was doing some kind of circus trick and appeared out of nowhere without a sound. One of the waiters told me he'd done time at the youth center for joyriding, and I couldn't help it—I started to imagine him trolling the back lanes of the old neighborhood, silent and quick, sliding in the front seat of the car as the family ate its angel-hair pasta and focaccia bread, backing out beneath the glow of the motion-detector light.

But that was before I really got to know him. Three months after we hooked up, he started following me around like a puppy waiting to be kicked.

"What's up with you?" I asked.

Then he started talking nonstop, a gushing vomit of words worthy of Lara herself. I knew his mother was from Argentina and he hadn't visited her in the loony bin for years. I knew his father was Filipino and had left when Mannie was two. I knew his best friend's mother, the saintly Betty, had taken him under her wing and kept him off the street. But that was it. I didn't want to know more. Why do people feel the need to trade their family histories just because they're trading bodily fluids?

Turns out his father had suddenly called Mannie after sixteen years and messed with his head. This guy, Eduardo or something, told him he'd met Mannie's mother in ESL classes and it had been love at first sight.

She was ten years older, a hot-to-trot former rich girl who still acted like she wasn't poor, and Eduardo decided to hell with his disapproving Catholic family. They moved in together, had a kid, and then she started coming unglued. Sometimes she wouldn't get out of bed for weeks, and other times she'd get caught walking out of grocery stores, cart loaded up and no receipt. It wasn't long before Eduardo was out of there, marrying a nice Filipino girl who sang at weddings.

"You have to understand," he told Mannie. "I have my own family now, and they wouldn't understand. But I think about you, and I wanted to know you're okay."

"What a tremendous prick," I said to Mannie when I found out.

But Mannie only shook his head. "No. You don't know what it's like to live with her."

I would've understood if he was fricking furious, but he wasn't. For a couple of weeks he just sulked, acting like he wanted something from me but had no idea what. And then, just like that, it was over. He didn't bring up Eduardo again—didn't even bring up poor, dead, saintly Betty for a while, which was nice.

Because no one had messed with Mannie's head the way that woman had. The world's problems will not be solved if we all go back to the bush and start picking our own berries, and you can't keep blaming your own problems on stuff that happened a hundred years ago. And Mannie is not one of the Indian Brotherhood just because he can pass.

Still, things were bearable until a few days ago, when Mannie quit the pizza place and started sitting around in the pawnshop recliner all day, playing *Grand Theft Auto*. And the other night, Warren brought home a girl who looked like she'd be found dead in a ditch sometime soon, and it was enough to make me want to crawl back to Ray on my hands and knees and vow to drown the Little Alien in a toilet. But I know how stubborn Ray can be—stubborn enough to pick himself up and dust himself off every single time, to keep promising to love them through better and through worse, to keep luring new investors for restaurant after restaurant, nightclub after nightclub.

"What's your plan?" I asked Mannie yesterday. "How are we going to eat?"

But he kept pouting and playing, ignoring me, just like his big, scary warrior buddy, Warren. Until last night when I got home from Olef and Helga's.

"Warren's gone," he said. "He had to bugger off for a while."

Mannie was still sitting in the recliner, but in the dark. The TV was nothing but a blank black screen. "From now on," he said, "I'm a changed man. I'm going to have a kid. This is no place for a kid."

I turned on the light. "No shit."

★ ✳ ★

Now, I open the bathroom door and he's standing right there, waiting.

"What?" I say.

"Nothing. You were just in there a long time."

The elastic in his underwear is saggy, and I can make out the top of his pubic hair. His stomach is perfectly flat, and before I can stop myself, I reach out and touch it. It's hard and smooth and amazing.

"I'm going to have stretch marks," I say. "It's not fair."

He cups both hands around the bump like he's about to shoot a hoop. "You're beautiful."

I know he's horny and full of shit. I know I'm constipated, I have morning breath, my fingers are swollen pork sausages. But I let him spill it. I let him tell me about the time Betty gave him his traditional name, how he is finally a changed man. I let him rub my feet in bed, let him coo at the bump, let him rest his head wherever he wants.

"I feel him, I feel him kicking," he says. "Hello. Hello, little Little Bear."

The next day, Denise wastes no time and sets up another interview. I take a nap in the afternoon, and I dream about Faye again, only Jill is there this time, and we're still kids. Jill is maybe fourteen, back when Lara called her "horsey-looking" when she wasn't around and her favorite lunch was sugar-and-banana sandwiches. She isn't a big-time model yet, hasn't sworn off all white foods. Hasn't couriered me a supersize suitcase full of her best fashionista shit, with no note, not a word, so that I know something is very wrong.

In my dream, Jill is brushing Faye's hair. "It's so strong," she says. "No split ends. You could do hair product, you know. You don't have to be tall. It doesn't matter."

"Faye is a musician," I say. "She's going to play in the symphony."

Faye rolls her eyes.

"Faye's adopted," I say. "She was born in China."

"That's so exotic," Jill says. "Exotic is hot right now, you know."

Faye's mother appears in the room, like a mama lion ready to pounce. "What on earth are you doing?"

Then the dream is over. I hear Mannie in the other room, breathing hard. He is counting push-ups to himself, something that normally makes me horny. But the Little

Alien is awake now too, getting out his knives, and I still feel like a kid, I'm still with Jill, back when we hung out all the time.

When the stepsibs came to visit, Ray was always keen to show off his only boy, Jill's brother, Thomas, so Jill and I were on our own. She taught me how to put in a tampon before I even got my period. She showed me how to extend my lashes with Vaseline. She could tell Lara to chill out without upsetting her.

Mannie comes in and crawls slowly toward me on the bed.

"You stink," I say.

He licks my earlobe. "You used to like it."

I push him away even though the licking has sort of worked. Part of me wants nothing more than for him to slide his finger between my legs. "What are we going to do for money?" I ask.

He puts his hands behind his head and stares up at the ceiling like there're fluffy clouds up there sailing through a blue sky. "Don't you worry about nothing. I got it covered."

"Anything," I say. "Don't worry about *anything*."

He lights up a joint and keeps watching the clouds. "Yeah, exactly."

"How?" I ask.

"How what?" he asks.

The Little Alien starts to hiccup, and suddenly I'm hungry, as if the secondhand smoke is giving me the munchies. "How do you have it covered?"

"Warren owed me," he says. "I got almost a thousand."

"What about when that's gone?" I ask.

He reaches over and brushes his fingers against my cheek. "Don't worry, babe. Your daddy's not the only one who can provide."

I roll out of bed instead of kneeing him in the balls for being such a dumbass. I eat some sugary O's, leave Jill behind and climb into the van with Denise. We pick up Faye to meet Lisa and Chris, and just one look tells me their profiles make perfect sense.

Lisa wears her hair butch-short and likes hiking and mystery novels. Chris is neatly bald, wearing pleated pants and a pinky ring. He likes hiking and jazz.

"You guys have only been married for a year," I say. "You haven't known each other all that long. How can you assure me your marriage is going to last?"

They look almost offended, are obviously not as hungry as Olef and Helga. They offer tea and coffee and that's it.

"We met late," Chris finally says. "But being more mature, we knew exactly what we wanted."

Lisa touches his hand for effect, but there is no way these two are getting it on. She has fag hag written all over her.

"We're ready to be parents now more than ever before in our lives."

If they start off cool, though, they eventually warm up, as if it takes them awhile to remember I have their fate in my hands.

They laugh at their spotless house, tell me they're more than ready for the drooling mess of a kid. They say they've researched daycares and found the best. They assure me they're prepared for any kind of presence I'd like in the child's life.

Back in the van, I ask Faye, "What's your bet? Do you think they have no idea they're both gay or are they just BFFs playing house for convenience?"

She stares back at me with those oh-so-wise, oh-so-black eyes. "You seem to be enjoying this."

"What do you mean?" I ask. "I'm just trying to lighten things up. Everyone's so tense."

Denise is already pulling away from the curb, but she slams on the brakes. She glares back at me like I've just blown a fart and added to the stink of her beater. "This is a serious thing, Bev."

"You think I don't know that?" I say. "It's my kid we're talking about."

"Forget it," Faye says. She sounds like her mother. "Let's just go."

We drive without a word until Faye breaks the silence. "When's the next interrogation?"

★ ✶ ★

The next day, Faye comes along again and we meet Charlie and Sid, who I also thought were gay when I first saw their file. But "Charlie" is actually short for Charlene, who turns out to be one very hot grade-five teacher. She looks like she is probably half black, with the kind of smooth latte skin and firm ass that little boys have their first wet dreams about. Sid isn't half bad either. He teaches phys ed and probably whitens his teeth. They have a brand-new house just outside the city that doesn't even have a lawn yet. Sid apologizes for the mucky slush on our way in, and I can tell he will do it again on our way out.

There are store-bought cookies and little wrapped candies on the coffee table. We go through the usual routine of questions.

"I guess my only concern," I say, "is that there's no reason you two might not have a baby of your own. Is that right?"

Charlie looks at Sid like she's begging him to field this one.

"Well, that's true," Sid says. "So far, no one has told us there's a significant medical reason why we're not getting pregnant. But we have a lot of love to give."

After she's had some time to think, Charlie jumps in. "We work with kids who aren't our own every day. We know how easy it is to find yourself loving a child if your heart is open. I'm sure we would love our adopted child just as easily and just as much as any possible natural offspring."

She says this in a way that makes you want to believe it.

Back in the van, Denise mutters that her new suede boots are caked with muck. Faye does up her seat belt and closes her eyes.

"I liked them," I say, "but they don't feel exactly right."

"Listen, honey," Denise says, trying so hard to be motherly I can tell she's ready to lose it. "Maybe we need to go through your options again. You need to feel sure."

"I'm sure," I say, "just not about them."

Faye's eyes remain closed. "Why?"

I remember a game she and I played as kids. We would answer a question with another question until we couldn't stand it anymore.

"Do you ever wish you weren't an only child?" I ask her.

Faye opens her eyes and appears to think, as if she's never considered this before. "Why?"

"Can you just answer the question, please?"

"No," she says, "not really," and I have my answer.

That night, I dream that I wake up and Mannie and Faye are standing over me.

"Give us the baby," Faye says.

"Forget it," I say. The Little Alien kicks so hard that you can see his foot bulge through my skin.

"See?" Mannie says. "He wants to leave." He's hiding something behind his back, which could very well be a knife.

"Get out of here," I say. "It's mine."

Mannie leans in close, looking at me the same way he looks when he's at the wheel of one of his SUVs—like he might lose control any second. "Give it," he says.

I lick my lips slowly, to show I'm not afraid. "You two wouldn't even know each other without me."

They both slink away, and I see Mannie is clutching a little hippo stuffie.

All weekend, I can't seem to get that stupid little hippo, soft and adorable and the color of storm clouds, out of my mind.

In the van on Monday, I read out the highlights of Will and Helen's file for Faye. Denise isn't entirely sure where she's going and keeps mumbling to herself.

"He's the assistant deputy minister for Culture, Heritage and Citizenship," I read. "She runs her own graphic design studio called Red Eye Inc. So she works from home, blah, blah, blah, more about their work. They met at a wedding and got married in their mid-thirties. He says she fills his day with energy and curiosity and fiercely loyal love. She says he makes her laugh and wears his heart on his sleeve. Reason for adoption? She had early menopause and so they have no chance of getting pregnant. They are ready to have an ongoing relationship with the child's biological family but would like to be able to determine when and how communication or contact occurs, based on the evolving best interests of the child."

"Jubilee," Faye pipes up. "I think you want to take Jubilee."

Denise brakes too hard but manages to get into the turning lane. We get lost for a while, driving around another neighborhood full of old houses and even older trees, except it's called Wildwood instead of River Heights. There are fewer shops and cafés around, as if you're in the country in the city. By the time we pull up to Will and Helen's, we're a good twenty minutes late.

Their house is just across the street from the river, pale yellow stucco with a red door that's rounded on the top. Along the sidewalk, little green tips are peeking up from the yellow grass. I try to remember which flowers bloom so early.

"Look," Faye says. "Tulips."

Both Will and Helen greet us at the door. She's tall, with long frizzy hair and just a bit of lipstick. He's taller, but his posture is terrible. The profile said he runs daily, but I bet he was always picked last in gym class.

Inside, there are paintings everywhere: on the walls, on the fireplace mantel, in the bookshelves. The coffee table is covered with books that look read and not just for show. There are bakery cinnamon buns and jam-filled cookies. Denise has coffee, Faye has bottled water, and I have cranberry juice. When it's time to get down to business, I try to think of a question and come up blank.

I point at the guitar propped up by the couch. "Do you play?"

Helen opens her eyes wide in pretend horror. "Oh, he tries. He threatened to put on a performance for you to show we're musical."

He smiles and takes off his glasses, the kind with no frames. He squeezes Helen's knee but looks at me. "She gently talked me out of it. You might say I'm a beginner."

"Faye plays the cello," I say.

They both turn to Faye at the same moment. "Yeah?" Helen says. "It's such a beautiful instrument."

Faye manages her heart-not-really-in-it smile. She is trying to sit with her feet tucked under her butt in a wooden rocking chair, and it's not working very well. "I used to," she says. "I mean, I'm taking a break."

Will leans back and crosses his arms, like he approves of this news. "Well, that's the great thing. Instruments are just like languages. You can always pick them up again later on."

I sip my juice. Nothing in the room matches, but it all seems to go together. Shabby chic, Lara would call it. Above the love seat where they're sitting, there is a huge oil painting that is nothing but blue-green swirls. If you look at it long enough, it starts to become the sea. The Little Alien delivers one good kick, then flutters a little near my belly button, like it's playing a drum roll with its tiny hands.

"Bev?" Denise asks. She doesn't seem impatient, just confused.

I push a book aside to make room for my juice glass. "I'm done," I say. "This feels right."

Will and Helen look at each other, uncomfortable for the first time. They think I'm joking.

"Really," I say. "You two. I pick you guys."

Denise clears her throat and pulls at her sleeves. "Okay then. Okay. You're ready to move forward, Bev?"

I tap the file on my lap. "I've read up. This is it. Let's get things rolling."

None of them are quite sure what to do. Suddenly it's like I'm the only adult in the room. I have to ask Denise to schedule a time to sign papers, have to ask Will and Helen where they put our coats. Helen manages to recover just before we leave and wraps up cinnamon buns to go.

Back in the van, Denise starts folding up the map. Faye and I leave the front passenger seat empty and sit behind Denise like she's driving us to kindergarten. Faye can't seem to get her seat belt done up. "What do you think?" I ask her.

She keeps jamming away, but still no telltale *click*. "You've obviously made up your mind."

"Okay," I say, "but I want to know what you think."

She throws her head back and talks to the roof of the car. "We barely talked to them. They seemed good. They seemed happy and successful. You don't need me here to tell you that."

Denise pulls away with the map still unfolded beside her and Faye still unclicked.

"Do you ever wish you could meet your birth mother?" I ask.

Faye is still staring at the ceiling. "It doesn't matter. My parents flew halfway across the world to avoid the issue. There's no point thinking about it."

Denise turns at the first stop sign and slows down, like she might get lost again. "I'm sure that's not the only reason they chose China," she says.

"But would you want to meet her if you could?" I ask.

"No," Faye says, almost a whisper. "I don't know. There's no point thinking about it."

Good ol' rational Faye. Deep down, she knows she has no reason to be pissed off—she came with me of her own free will. Because when it comes down to it, even when we were kids I never had to do much more than twist her rubber arm.

★ ★ ★

Mannie is waiting when I get home. "So?"

"It's done," I say. "They live in Wildwood."

"What do you mean, it's done?"

I close my eyes and realize I'm dizzy with hunger. "Come on, Mannie, don't play dumb. I'm getting the papers. I like the vibe I get from them."

Mannie rests his hand on the bump, and for once the Little Alien cooperates. It doesn't move—in fact, it hasn't moved in a few hours.

"What about me?" he asks. "Don't I get a say?"

This is it. There's no more skirting around things, no more letting little Mannie think for one more minute that he is going to make me an honest woman with a homestead in the bush. It's time to break through that thick skull and let the bony bits fall where they may.

"This isn't about you, Mannie," I say. "It's about what's best for our kid."

He shakes his head like a three-year-old who's refusing to go to bed. "I should have a say."

I take his hand and put it against my cheek the way he likes. "Don't you trust me? You say you love me, but don't you trust me?"

He keeps shaking his head. "I don't care who they are. My kid belongs with me."

"Mannie, that's not going to happen," I say. "I'm not going through all this so my kid can grow up in this dump."

It's hard to tell if I'm getting through, but I keep on. "I have final say because I haven't slept for more than three hours straight in months. I think I'm getting hemorrhoids. You want to be there in the delivery room? Fifty bucks you'll faint."

He pulls his hand away. "Why didn't you just get rid of him then?"

"You don't know it's a he."

"Whatever," he says. "You know what I mean. He. She. It. That's what you said. You said you were going to get an abortion."

My stomach growls and Mannie's hand returns to the bump. I have nothing left to say. I'm out of answers. I'm suddenly so tired I can hardly sit up.

"Bev," he says. "I've never known anyone like you before. You're not afraid of anything, and you don't take any shit. Betty didn't take any shit either. And she wasn't afraid, even when she was dying."

Please, Mannie, I think. Please stop talking.

"She would've liked you," he says.

Please, Mannie, oh please.

"If you love me," I say, "you'll help me."

"You are such a bitch," he says and walks out the door as if he has somewhere to go.

After Mannie leaves, my stomach rumbles like a semi-trailer full of marbles. I lie down and drift in and out of sleep, and I can't tell if I'm dreaming or remembering.

I'm back in the house we lived in before Montrose, the little rental by the overpass. I'm not in school yet, and in the morning Lara takes me to the public pool up the street and teaches me to float. At lunchtime we take a cab to the restaurant, and Ray introduces us as "his girls." I eat garlic toast and the bartender makes me a drink with a cherry. I feel so tired, I lie down in a booth and fall asleep. The next thing I know, Ray is carrying me in from his car, cradling my cheek in his hand.

"What the hell is the matter with her?" he asks.

Lara is there whenever I wake up. She looks terrible—unwashed hair, lips that disappear into her face. She makes me drink water. Sometimes Ray comes in, and they sit together in the half-light, one person with two heads.

Then I'm sitting propped up by pillows, and Ray is carrying a TV into my room. Lara watches movies with me, anything I want, the one about the mermaid who gives up her voice to get the prince, over and over. She teaches me how to play Go Fish and lets me win. Ray doesn't let me win. He brings me popcorn that Lara won't let me eat.

He brings a unicorn the size of a big dog. I name him Horny, and they laugh and laugh and I don't know why.

My phone rings, and now I know it isn't a dream, but a memory. It really happened, before Mannie ever loved me, before Faye ever came over, when Ray still thought he was going to franchise the restaurant, go national, maybe even the States, and Lara still believed in till death do you part.

"Christ," Ray said afterward. "Hepatitis. It was that pool. It's a goddamn germ factory."

SEVEN

Later in the week, Denise phones to say Helen would like to help with anything she can. "You're not obliged to involve her at this point. It's up to you." Mannie glares, as if my phone call is messing with his concentration. I'm starting to think he's two different people. When he's on a roll, there's no stopping him—you can see it in his hands, the way they clench and relax, clench and relax. He's full of crazy plans, ready to try anything, ready to take our lives in those stronger-than-they-look fists. But when he crashes, he crashes. Since he stopped talking to me, he's spent all his time getting high and pretending to race little pretend cars. He keeps the volume up and crashes so much, I can't believe I ever got into a car with him.

"What kind of help?" I ask.

"Well, there's a range of things," Denise says. "Like your next OBGYN appointment is tomorrow, right? She could take you if you want."

So the next morning, Helen picks me up in her silver hybrid. "Do you live on your own?" she asks.

I left Mannie snoring on the futon and waited downstairs at the curb. If Helen's freaked out by the seedy downtown apartment, she doesn't show it.

"No," I say. "It's my boyfriend's place."

She takes a breath, like she wishes she smoked so she could pause for a puff.

I roll down the window a bit. It really smells like a Winnipeg spring now, that mix of wet grit and snow mold and dog shit. Mannie's cologne, scrambled eggs, nail polish—they all make me want to stop breathing these days, but the smell of April is okay, that messy, sweet stench of everything waking up.

At the doctor's office, we wait more than half an hour in a jam-packed row of crappy chairs. When we're finally called in, she grips her magazine like it's a bible that will somehow tell her what to do.

"Aren't you coming?" I ask.

I change into the hideous blue paper gown while she waits outside. As the nurse weighs me, Helen pretends to read a poster about hypnobirthing.

The nurse is obviously off the boat from somewhere like Poland. She has a gold tooth and is always yelling at people over the phone.

"One houndred fifty-fife," she shouts at me. "Fife pounds seence last time."

I wave Helen over and whisper, "They make the gowns this color so we look like whales."

She laughs and seems to relax a little. "You look great."

Dr. Kohut introduces himself to Helen in a way that makes me think Denise must've got to him first. He seems to know exactly why Helen's here before we fill him in and eagerly pats the examining table, like he's calling a dog. "Well, let's get you up here, Bev, and see how that baby's doing."

He spreads the ice-cold jelly over my stomach and roams around with the wand until we hear the heartbeat. It's loud and fast, a steady hip-hop rhythm that fills the room. At the first appointment, back when I still fit into regular jeans, he said, "Just think: that same heart will beat for the rest of your baby's life." I wonder how many times he's said that in that same calm, confident way.

He leaves the wand there forever this time, and we're surrounded by the *thumpa-thumpa-thumpa-thump*, a tiny rave for three, until finally he wipes the goo off and starts to poke around.

Helen wipes her eyes as he starts pressing around my groin. His fingers are bony and cold. "How's the pain?"

He always asks this like he's a waiter asking me about my dinner—*How's the steak, miss?* "It comes and goes," I say, "but if labor is worse than the shooting needles in my ass, you're going to have to put me out."

He makes a weird hiccup that I think is supposed to be a laugh. "Well, the baby's still breech. The pain is coming from his feet around your pelvis and sciatic. We may very well be scheduling a C-section if he doesn't start moving."

He takes my blood pressure. Helen is looking a little dazed, but she smiles at me like we're sharing a secret. *I know*, her smile seems to say. *He's a dink.*

Dr. Calm and Confident makes a cartoon worry face, eyebrows stitched, mouth turned way down. "Your blood pressure is up."

He pumps the cuff up again until it feels like my elbow is choking. He keeps frowning. "We'd really like to get you to at least thirty-six weeks, Bev. That's our goal. But we're going to have to get those numbers down. We're probably looking at bed rest."

I wonder what "we" he's talking about. Helen folds her hands together in her lap and nods as if taking mental notes. He keeps talking, but I don't hear much because I'm looking at Helen's fingers. They're thin and long, with short-clipped nails and perfect cuticles. I remember Jill

always used red or burgundy when she gave me a mani-
cure. "We have fat knuckles," she said, "so we need bold
colors as an offset."

Back in the hybrid, Helen waits until we're out of the
parkade to debrief. I know exactly what she's going to say.

"Bev, you know we're here to help any way we can.
You just have to tell us what we can do to help you
through this."

I roll down the window and stare out like I'm embarrassed just to be having this conversation. "I'm okay."

"Please, Bev," Helen says. "You need to let us know if
you need help."

I sigh. People always want to look after me. Even though
Ray ignored her when Jill came to visit, even though Lara
wished she would go away, Jill still wanted to look after
me. When I was a snotty little kid, she was always making
me banana-and-sugar sandwiches, straightening my hair,
buying me crap from the dollar store. Then later, she'd
send me clothes, expensive clothes, even though she didn't
know what size I was anymore. "My boyfriend, Mannie,"
I say. "He quit his job."

Helen brightens up like I just handed her a bouquet
of roses. "Well, can we help with the groceries? I could go
shopping, drop something by."

She doesn't give me a chance to answer. "But that's
presumptuous, isn't it? I don't know what you'd like."

She pulls four twenties out of her purse. "Your boyfriend—what's his name?"

Denise has made it clear that Will and Helen are to cover legal costs but provide no "gifts" of any kind. "Mannie," I say.

"Mannie. Will he go shopping for you?"

"Of course," I say.

Upstairs, I turn on the light and see him still flat on his stomach in bed. I throw the money at him, and it floats down onto the mess of covers like dead leaves.

"Go buy some food," I say. "I'm supposed to rest."

He shields his eyes like I'm the sun. "You okay?"

"Yeah," I say, "I'm super. That's why the doctor says I have to spend the next two months in bed."

He throws off the covers, sends the money flying, starts fishing for some underwear under the bed. "Since when?"

"Since now," I say.

He stands up, naked and still wobbly from sleep. He smells like armpits and weed. I let him take my hand, sit me on the bed, pull me against his smooth, hard chest, and the whole time I'm thinking, If he weren't such a pussy, he would've kicked me out long ago.

That night I dream about Faye and my sister Jill again. Jill is giving Faye reddish highlights just like Helen's.

When Jill takes the towel off, Faye looks ridiculous, a tiger with orange and black stripes. Lara walks in and starts laughing, a mean, stupid laugh. I wake up sweating and remember something I didn't even know I'd forgotten.

It's the Saturday morning Lara found out that Ray was getting it on with his napkin supplier. The cutlery drawer is open, and she's throwing forks at him. Faye and I make a beeline out of there before she gets to the butter knives— or worse. We try to ignore them by playing hairdresser and get carried away. Faye goes home with the worst bowl cut in history, and the next day, her mom rings the doorbell before Ray and Lara are out of bed. I'm on the floor behind the love seat, watching TV, hidden from sight. She pretends she doesn't notice that Lara is in her bathrobe, tells her Faye won't be coming over to the house again. Lara asks why and Faye's mom says, "You better ask Bev that." Lara says she will, but she doesn't.

★★★

There are no more dreams after that, and the days start to blur together. Mannie brings me street-vendor-style pretzels, chocolate pudding packs, fruit punch, whatever I ask for. He moves the TV into our room and I watch shows about midget families and bitchy chefs. The Little Alien has its regular exercise routine: punching, kicking, elbowing, poking, but no somersaults. When it's worn out, I pass out like I'm the one in training.

Every few days, the public health nurse appears like a nasty fairy godmother, chokes my arm with the blood-pressure cuff, frowns, tells me to stay put. Sometimes she brings little orange pills for the pain. Denise comes by with papers and tells me I need to be sure about what I'm signing. She says Mannie scrawled his signature without looking at her or the fine print, and she takes this as a sign that he's a disinterested prick.

It turns out I have up to ten days after the birth of the Little Alien to change my mind. I could tell Will and Helen that the groceries were appreciated, but they'll have to pursue their hopes and dreams elsewhere. I pretend to read every word carefully, then tell Denise I'm of sound mind and send her away.

She keeps coming back, though, with questions and files and legal dockets. *Would you allow Will and Helen in the delivery room?* Whatever. *Would you like to send birthday presents?* No. *Would you like annual pictures?* No. *Have you notified the father of the impending adoption?* Yes. *Are you sure you don't want him as part of the process?* Yes.

I just want everyone to leave me alone with my wretchedness, like Lara when her weight had ballooned and she'd spend weeks in her room, blinds closed, mourning her former slim self. When I lived on the coast, whales would beach themselves all the time, and there'd always be the same cadre of do-gooders who would wring their hands and try to save the thing. I lost my virginity to a guy who put on headphones and listened to their calls in his spare time, and I swear he would've had sex with one if he could. I start to think that Mr. Creepy Whale Guy would regret having dumped me now, because as the days go by, I become more and more like one of those poor, dumb piles of blubber, waiting for something or someone to put me out of my misery.

At some point, Faye texts me. what's up with Will and Helen? R U OK?

I don't feel like dealing with Faye or anyone else. It's enough with the Little Alien weighing on me, craving starch and fat, dancing around on my nerves until I have to scream bloody murder. Even Mannie starts to stay away, afraid I'll scratch his face off with my ragged nails if he brings the wrong brand of juice.

Then one day, the nasty nurse chokes my arm, frowns, makes a call and the gang is suddenly all there, surrounding me. Denise. Helen. Will. Dr. Kohut.

"Your blood pressure still isn't cooperating," says the good doctor, like he's ready to fail my arteries in preschool. "You did a good job, Bev. Nearly thirty-five weeks. But there's an ambulance waiting, okay, Bev? We're going to go check things out."

I purposely did not think about this day, but I know this: This is not the way I would've imagined it if I'd imagined it.

Helen reaches over and takes my hand. "Should we call someone? Would you like us to call Faye?"

Faye? I realize how strange it must seem to them that I have no one.

"Right," I say. "Yeah. I'll text Faye."

The hospital is just as dumpy as when I went for the ultrasound and some sniffer was puking near the front entrance. This time, the sliding doors to the triage unit are stuck shut and we have to take a detour.

I let Will and Helen hold my elbows like I might faint at any moment, because really, I'm having trouble focusing. Because baby brain is a scientific fact. Because I am not ready for this, not ready to let this wave take me, not yet.

"We need you to tell us what you'd prefer," Helen says. "We can stay with you the whole time, or we can stay close by, in the waiting room. Or you can send us home and call us later."

That's too many choices, I want to say. One of Ray's biggest ventures went belly-up because they tried to be everything to everyone. The menu was seven pages long, two of them listing nothing but mixed drinks.

"Whatever," I say. "Stay, go. I don't care."

For the first time in my life, I'm happy to follow orders. I slip into a whale-blue gown, and a grumpy nurse with happy faces all over her uniform attaches little electrodes to the bump. Helen sits beside me, trying to look comfortable in the shit chair, and Will crouches beside her like a chimp. They look like they could be my parents, and I wonder if they know this or if they're both too busy watching the little needle scratching out each heartbeat.

I have no idea how much time passes before Will gets up, his legs half-asleep, before he soldiers on, wobbly-kneed, helping me as best he can into a wheelchair, pretending not to notice my gown gaping, wheeling me down the hall, slow and steady, his loafers softly squeaking as we go. Helen's hand is on my shoulder, as if I might escape. I look down at my slippers. They are so huge, I'd have to flop away, no longer a whale but an enormously pregnant blue penguin.

I am on the operating table, and someone, a nurse maybe, is telling me about the needle that will numb my bottom half, and I feel like laughing, because I have always been good with needles. I know when the hurt will begin and when it will end, and it suddenly hits me that there will be no labor pains, no hyperventilating, no pushing and sweating. No wonder all the celebrities do it like this.

I lie back, let the numbness take hold. For the first time in months, my back does not hurt. Will and Helen are somewhere, I don't know where. I can hear them murmuring to each other, like lovebirds in class. The light is bright, and I close my eyes. In my mind, I see Will's squeaky loafers, Helen's deep-red patent-leather ankle boots, my stupid hospital slippers. That's what I see at a time like this—shoes.

I keep my eyes closed. After Jill's overdose, they ran a full-body shot, some year-old magazine cover. She was wearing a belted wool coat and giant fur hat and strappy silver heels. "That photo is ridiculous," Lara had said. "She deserved better."

Ray flew Jill's body home and had her funeral at the St. Boniface basilica, even though he's probably the worst Catholic in all of history. The impressive old church had burned down years earlier, leaving nothing of the original building but a massive stone edifice. They had rebuilt the new structure low and modern but left the edifice towering in front. As we followed the coffin out, Lara had pointed up at the stone. "See that big circle up there? There used to be a stained-glass rose window set inside. Christ, it must've been fabulous."

I can feel the fall wind biting, I can see the big, round, fabulous hole framing nothing but cold blue sky.

Then there is tugging, lots of tugging, but no pain. Somewhere, someone is saying things calmly and confidently, but they're almost completely drowned out by something quieter—someone sniffling, probably Helen. The harder the tugging, the harder I squeeze my eyes, until there is a huge sucking release, and I panic. I see it held up, gooey and mauve. It is not red, not purple, but mauve. It isn't crying. It looks dead, but it can't be because it is peeing, a wee arc coming from a wee mauve penis. I shut my eyes tight again.

Someone squeezes my shoulder. "You did fantastic, Bev."

It's Helen. At first, I think she smells awful, but then I realize it must be the whole room that stinks, from a flood of fluids—blood, pee, snot, other things I don't want to talk about.

"We've got ourselves a boy, Bev. You did it. You did it."

It's Will. He's the one who was sniffling.

Helen strokes my cheek. "He's tiny, but so far, so good. They'll be taking him to intensive care to be safe."

"I'm tired," I say.

"Of course," she says. "You rest, sweetie. You stay still. They're going to stitch you up now."

Only Lara has ever called me "sweetie," and I always hated it. But somehow it's okay coming from Helen, maybe because she doesn't say it like she wants something. She already has what she wants.

"You're almost done," Will says. "You shout if you need anything, okay?"

If they think I'm going to open my eyes, they are mistaken.

"You guys, go," I say. "Please. I'm okay."

Will's shoes squish away as I'm tugged and stitched, and I don't even know I've been asleep until Helen is brushing my cheek again.

"Bev. He's still here, just for a moment. Do you want to see him?"

I can hear snuffling, like the inbred cat who lived next door to us in Vancouver. Its nose was so pushed in, you could open a can of tuna and it wouldn't smell a thing.

I shake my head.

There is a long pause. Helen is probably wondering if she should ask again.

"Okay," she says. "You rest. You rest, sweetie."

When I wake up, a nurse is wheeling a tray to my bed. She has pink bunny rabbits on her uniform, but she is more of a gorilla. Her mustache makes Denise's look like peach fuzz.

"Dinnertime," she says, all friendly. "You must be hungry, no?"

It smells like gravy and Jell-O, and I realize I'm hungry enough to eat my own arm. I sit up a little, and the pain rips through me like someone with a voodoo doll has it in for me.

"Easy," Gorilla says. "We'll do this slow. Okay, sweetie? You've got stitches there, so we need to go slow."

She uncovers a hot beef sandwich and a salad of iceberg lettuce and cucumbers. She scoops dressing out of the little packet with a fork. She opens my milk and sticks the straw in. She does everything but start chewing my food for me—the gorilla with a heart of gold.

I try the beef, but my tongue isn't nearly as interested as my stomach was. The meat tastes bland and chewy. The lettuce is a little brown around the edges, and the cucumber is not even peeled. I take a bite of a tea biscuit, which is the exact same shape as a hockey puck.

I take a sip of milk and give the Gorilla the thumbs-up. Why do I care whether she thinks I like her shitty food?

She turns to go and I almost ask her to hold on, to stay for just another minute. But Faye appears in the doorway, holding up her palm like an Indian in a movie saying, "How."

She's wearing the same jeans she always wears, but her jacket is new, a red spring pea coat that makes her hair look blacker than black. She comes to the foot of the bed, then stops as if I might be contagious. "How are you?"

I poke at the salad, looking for something edible. "Sore."

"I saw him for a sec through the door," she says. "They called him Olivier."

So much for small talk. I take another sip of milk and nod.

"You were sleeping," she says. She keeps her hands in her pockets. They're sewn on an angle and have yellow trim. "He's in intensive care. Helen says he's five pounds, but he's breathing on his own. His lungs are good."

I shove some beef into my mouth and chew, nodding the whole time.

"Have you?" she asks.

I swallow. "Have I what?"

"Have you seen him?"

I start drinking again as if dying of thirst. I shake my head.

I can tell Faye is picking her fingers in her pockets. "Will you?" she says.

I wipe my face with a napkin. "I think it's best if I don't."

Faye nods, too long, like she's already thinking of something else. "Why did you ask me to come?"

I straighten out the tin foil and cover up the sad excuse for beef. *Let us pray for this dead, tasteless cow.* "I don't know. Everyone else had bailed."

She takes an elastic out of her pocket and pulls her hair back into a ponytail. It makes her look about ten years old. "I had an exam," she says. "That's why it took so long."

I lean back and remember the voodoo again. Maybe Mannie is going after my guts now that his precious son is safe and sound.

"You okay?" Faye asks.

"Yeah," I say. "It's just the stitches."

Her eyebrows make a little upside down *V*. She looks like a concerned ten-year-old. "I have another one tomorrow," she says. "I haven't even looked at my notes."

This makes me laugh, which hurts like a bugger. "Good little Faye. You should go study."

She looks slightly pissed off at this, but I start to shoo her away.

"Go," I say. "Go. I don't want you to fail because of me."

"Let me know if you need anything," she says.

I can't tell if she's being polite or if she really gives a shit. Maybe she doesn't know either.

"You bet," I say. "Go study. Give 'em hell."

After she's gone, the orderly comes in for the tray and I fake sleep. I'm tired of talking, of trying to stay one step ahead. The last thing I need is Helen hovering, asking me what I want.

With the tray gone, with nothing but me and the whale-blue gown, I notice my stomach for the first time. Just like that, I am no longer hard and round, but bloated and flabby. Just like that, I am alone. And it's strange, but it's like my hands feel lost without the bump. After all those weeks in bed, I got used to resting them there on my portable TV table. I got used to feeling the punches against my palms letting me know that it was still alive, asking for nothing but some sugary O's.

I poke at my layer of flab even though it hurts— nothing but blubber. For a minute, I think of picking up the phone and calling Lara, but I decide it's not worth it. She would only blab on about the kid being an Aries or a Gemini or whatever the hell sign the middle of May is, and I would hate myself for being such a suck.

Lara went through a phase when she thought every single dream she had must mean something important. I was eleven, held hostage because Ray was going through bankruptcy and not up for even a visit, and even then, I knew she was blowing smoke. Because I'm not stupid. I don't believe in all that New Age shit, don't believe in anything except my instincts.

Thirty-five weeks doesn't seem like a long time, but it is. There were months of the Little Alien tossing around my cookies, then more months of him bearing down on my every move, of jabs that stole my sleep and kick-started my dreams, that reminded me he was still there, that he still needed me.

Then just like that, he is gone and I'm light as air again, a helium balloon that some kid lost at a birthday party. I know this feeling well, which is good, because my instincts will know exactly what to do.

Denise will come. She will be motherly or business-like, a buddy or a fellow screw-up, depending on her mood. I will not renege on my contract. I will ask not to see Helen and Will again. Because, unlike Mannie, I am not stupid. I will let the Little Alien take off to its home planet, that gingerbread house in Wildwood where flowers poke up through the snow and people call their kid Olivier without sounding like assholes. I will remember that even though school was a joke, I've learned a few things.

I will hail a cab, and it won't matter as much that it smells like bad aftershave and stinky feet, because I am alone again.

Ray will pay the cabbie and say, *Look who the cat dragged in.*

He will talk a hard line, tell me I have to start in the kitchen, work my way up, just like he did. But he will let me waitress, give me the best tables even though it pisses off his staff, start grooming me because everyone else has bailed and I'm all he has.

I can already see him sitting there in his office, tilting back in the leather chair that looks like a first-class plane seat. He'll look me over, take note of the flab around the belly.

So, it's my girl, he'll say. *You look pretty good. Are you good?*

He'll say it loud and cheery, in a way that makes it seem like he cares.

PART THREE

Mannie

EIGHT

If there's one thing I learned from my foster mother, Betty, it's that legal papers don't mean shit, especially if you had no choice but to sign. One look at those old First Nations' treaties and it doesn't take a genius to know someone is getting screwed. So I don't just sit around with a piano tied to my ass, as Betty liked to say.

I light up a joint and call the number I nabbed from Bev's phone. I don't hang up this time. "Is this Faye?"

It takes a second. "Yes. Who's this?"

"It's Mannie," I say. "We met before."

"Have you been calling me?" she asks. "Like, for a while? Have you been calling my cell?"

I consider the choices—yes or no, admit or deny. But she doesn't give me a chance.

"Whatever. It doesn't matter. What do you want, Mannie?"

"I need to see my kid," I say.

I get nothing. It sounds like she's outside, walking somewhere. Someone else is talking, and the birds are finally back in town for the summer, *chirp, chirp, chirping*.

"Yeah," she says. "Can you call back in ten minutes?"

She obviously wants to blow someone off before we talk, so I give her twelve, just to be safe. It's enough to relax a little, get a bit of a buzz on, which is good. When I call again, it's like she's in an echo chamber—a bathroom maybe, or a stairwell.

"Where's Bev?" she asks. "Does she know about this?"

I take a drag, stay nice and calm. "She's at Ray's. She won't talk to me."

I get nothing again. "Was it a boy or a girl?" I ask. "I bet you know."

There's a long pause, and the quiet is creepy, like a sound vacuum. "A boy," she says. "Olivier."

I can't help it. I start laughing. "Seriously? Does Ray know? He'd think that was so faggy. He'd fricking hate it."

Even as I'm saying this, I know I'm messing things up. I take another drag, get a grip. "Yeah, see, the thing is, I need to see it."

Nothing.

"I need to see him, Faye."

"You have to talk to Bev about that," she says.

When I first saw Bev's little uptight Chinese friend, I thought of what Betty used to say about my case worker: "Someone's got to pull that stick out of her ass."

"Did you hear what I said? She won't talk to me. She won't come to the phone. Ray says he's getting a restraining order, but he doesn't know shit about the law."

"I haven't talked to her either," Faye says. "Not since the hospital."

"Come on," I say. "Don't be a bitch. Do you know where my kid is?"

"No," she says. "I don't."

"Bullshit," I say. "You know."

"You both signed an agreement," she says. "You can't just show up at their door."

She so knows. "I don't want to go to any door. I just want to have a look."

Nothing.

"Do you know the street? Just tell me the street."

"I can't remember," she says. "And it doesn't matter. There's a written agreement that you both signed."

I laugh again, because I can't believe this shit. Betty is rolling in her grave because she can't believe it either. "That's my boy," I say. "I just want to see where he lives. That's all, man."

"I'm sorry," she says. "I need to go."

"I'll call back," I say. "Maybe you'll remember."

"Okay," she says. "Call back." Like she'll say just about anything to get rid of me.

★✶★

I give her two days. I'm so sure she won't pick up that the TV is still blaring when she does. It takes me a bit to find the remote and turn down the lame cop show and its sirens. I take it as a good sign that she doesn't hang up.

"What do you want from me?" she asks.

"So you've been to their house," I say. "You must've been."

Nothing.

"We don't need an address. I got a truck. You could just sort of show me the way. Just so I could see it. You know, the place where my kid is gonna grow up."

Then, just like that, she caves, like whatever loyalty she had to Bev was a house of cards.

★✶★

It's stinking warm for the last week of May, and I wonder if my kid has air-conditioning in his place. My madre was from Argentina, and she said the Canadian prairies had no real spring—one day it was winter and the next it was summer. She may have been crazy about most things, but now and then she had a point.

Betty's rusty red beater smells as bad as it looks, and for a minute I wonder whether little River Heights Faye will even get in when I pick her up. The duct tape on the passenger seat has worn away, leaving nothing but stringy glue and a gaping wound that looks like it should be oozing guts. The clock and the stereo have some wiring issues I haven't bothered to fix. Even the dream catcher hanging from the rearview mirror is looking a little tired, a few feathers and a couple of beads lost god-knows-where. Maybe Betty misses it and so her ghost comes in the night, taking it back bit by bit.

But I'm already late and Warren was in my face demanding cash as I went out the door and there's nothing I can do about the truck anyway. She either gets in or she doesn't.

I pull up in front of the hair salon with the giant scissors out front. She's huddled under the awning, deep in the corner behind the sign, like it's freezing out or she doesn't want to be seen. As soon as she spies me, though, she darts out and jumps in the cab.

She does up her seat belt and tries to close the glove compartment.

"The latch is tricky," I say. "This thing is a piece of shit, but I got my reasons for keeping her on the road."

She gives up. Luckily, her legs are so short that the gaping compartment door doesn't even graze her knees. Her calves are hairless, like mine. "No wonder you like to think you're an Abo," Bev said once. "Just like them, you're as silky smooth as a little girl." Bev had plenty of soft blond down in all the right places.

I forget to signal as I pull out, and some asshole honks.

If Faye notices, she doesn't show it. She looks straight ahead, all business. "Do you know the overpass on Pembina?"

"No sweat," I say.

She's so quiet, I can't stand it. She looks so small there beside me, so solemn, that if I were a cop, I'd pull us over as a possible pedophile and his victim.

"So what did Bev tell you about me?" I ask. "Did she say anything?"

She is gazing at my forearms as I drive. Bev used to lie in bed and trace my veins, say they looked like little rivers on a map. Faye looks away as if I've just said this out loud. "Not much. She said you were really into the idea of being a daddy."

I get out a sad-looking pack of gum from my pocket and wave it at her. There's two left, but she shakes her head. I drive with my wrists as I unwrap a piece, and she watches my arms again.

"I was just wondering," I say, "because Ray is a piece of goddamn work. He thinks I'm not good enough for his precious baby, but he's fine with getting rid of his own grandkid. He doesn't really give a shit about Bev. He just wants to tell her what to do."

Faye grabs the gum pack off my thigh and takes the last piece. Bev always says, "All women reserve the right to change their minds, so get used to it." I guess she's right.

"I don't know much about him," she says. "But he seemed like a pretty distant father."

I smack the steering wheel, then hit the brakes a little hard at an amber light. We're finally getting somewhere. "Exactly. Distant and dominating. That's Ray."

Faye chews mostly with her front teeth, as if she thinks her molars would be too big and mean up against that little stick of gum.

"Do you think I can get her back?" I ask.

She shrugs, a little kid who's just been asked, *Who did this?* "I have no idea. Like I said, I haven't even spoken to her since the hospital."

No matter how hard I try, I can't get a read on her. She helped Bev give up my kid, and now she's here, helping me. So where does that get me with little Chinese Faye? Nowhere.

I turn left at the private girls' school, where they're outside practicing field hockey with their pushed-down knee socks and pushed-up tits.

"I'll tell you what I do know," I say. "I have my rights."

We get to Pembina, head through the underpass with its lame-ass South End grafitti. A DIY frame shop comes up on our left. "This look familiar?" I ask.

She nods. "Turn left here."

I'm in the wrong lane and have to get over quick. Another asshole honks, and Faye closes her eyes for a second, then gives a little wave to the other driver. We head into a maze of tree-lined streets, past houses with pastel-stucco fronts and nothing but dandelions for lawns.

"This Wildwood," I say. "How far east does it go?"

She shrugs again, as if she has no idea which direction east is. *If women don't know something, it's just because we don't give a shit.* Another one of Bev's sayings.

"All the way to the river," Faye says.

All the way to the end of the road, a dead end—doesn't get much simpler than that. She points left, then left again. "Stop. That one there, with the bright-red door."

I hit the brakes but still have to put the truck in reverse, back up maybe fifteen feet. It's right across the street from the river, a house from a storybook. The doorway is an arch, and the windows are not flat but jut out in threes, like you could build a seat in them and while away your livelong day. A tree full of tiny pink flowers reaches over the front porch like a giant arm. Outside in the driveway, there's a high-end khaki stroller, but otherwise, there's no sign of life.

"It's a charming house," Faye says, so quietly I can hardly hear her. It's like she's forgotten I'm there and is talking to herself. "Those chokecherry petals on the grass—they look like pink snow."

I nod. "Do you think they're home?"

More shrugging, and I begin to wonder if this is a thing with her—a tiny body in a big hoodie trying to shrug herself down until she disappears, like a turtle.

"They left stuff in the yard," I say. "Who goes out and just leaves stuff there?"

"Maybe they think it's a safe neighborhood," she says.

I reach across to the glove compartment and fish out a joint. Some old parking tickets and a pair of broken sunglasses slide onto the floor, but she pretends not to notice.

My lighter is on its last legs and it takes three tries to get her going. Words cannot express how much I need the hit, and within seconds, I'm no longer about to scream bloody murder at uptight turtle Faye.

"That's stupid," I say. "No place is that safe."

I offer her a puff, just to be polite, not because I think she'll take it. But it's like with the gum. She holds up her hand at first—*no way, no thanks*—then ends up taking it anyway. She holds it very dainty, her fingers making a perfect little a-okay sign, and doesn't cough as much as I expected. She takes three hits, squinting her black eyes as she exhales, like when she decides to do something, she does it right.

"So Bev," I say, "she didn't tell me squat about you. You two go way back? You friends as kids?"

She leans back against the dirty headrest, looks chill for the first time. "Sort of. We were neighbors for a while. She lived across the street from the time we were five until we were eight."

The sun appears from behind a cloud, and I blow smoke into its rays. "No shit. You knew Bev way back then? What was she like?"

She lets her head flop toward me, really looks at me for the first time since she got in the truck. "The same."

This makes me laugh, makes me wonder if this girl is at all who I think she is. "So why were you two just *sort of* friends?"

She smiles like I've made a joke. Her right hand is still in the a-okay position, as if she's holding her own imaginary joint now. "Did I say that?"

"Yeah, you said you were *sort of* friends."

She nods, stops smiling. "Well, it was convenient for my parents to have me hang out at Bev's place all the time."

"What, they made you go?" I ask.

"No," she says, "no," but it's like she's talking to herself again. "It was just easier if I did. I'm an only child, and I think they were glad I had a friend. It was so easy to say,

Sure, go to Bev's. Isn't it nice a girl your age moved in? I've got a deadline. I'll be doing the crossword. Whatever. So when Bev finally crossed the line, my parents acted like she was the devil, even though it was just some hair. But it was just their guilt, their own stupid guilt."

So all it takes is some good-quality weed and the stick flies out of her ass. She's just like the rest of them, going on about the same shit girls go on about.

"Yeah?" I say. "Well, all I know is I'm going to be nothing like my folks. They were useless tits."

She finds this hilarious.

"I'm serious," I say.

She holds up her hands in surrender. "I believe you."

The perfume of the pink tree outside mixes with the sweet, smooth smell of the joint and turns Betty's stinking truck not half-bad. Any breeze has gone dead in the big leafy trees. A big dog starts barking like it means business.

She stares straight ahead. "Were your parents religious?"

I have to think for a second, make sure she said what I think she said. There really is no reading this girl. "Religious?"

"Yeah," she says. "Were they spiritual people? Did they go to church?"

Here, in front of my kid's house, the last thing I want to talk about is my crazy madre.

"My foster mom, Betty," I say, "she did the sweat and thanked the Creator and shit. She talked about the Circle and the Cycle, how we're all never-ending. She believed in dreams and said anyone who thought history moved in a straight line was a jackass."

Faye gives the dream catcher a little push with her finger, sending it swinging in the still air. "Okay, but Mannie is Spanish, right? Short for Emmanuel?"

"Yeah," I say. "But nobody ever calls me that."

"Right. But Emmanuel means 'God is with us.'"

"No shit?" I ask.

"No shit," she says. "Our cleaning lady, Tina—her son is named Emmanuel."

After that we just sit for a while, like it was with my buddy Nathan, Betty's youngest, when we were kids and could sit together without saying a single word.

Then her phone buzzes, and she makes no effort to hide the text. Mom still not talking. Dad sulking. Colm pale and depressed.

"I have to go," she says.

And I pretend I'm happy to take her whenever and wherever she asks, that it's the least I can do. I pretend that the truck's relentless stench isn't creeping back, pretend I don't care that the stroller in the driveway was fatigue khaki, expensive and ugly, instead of baby blue with maybe little yellow ducks printed on it.

NINE

It turns out my kid's street isn't a bad place to smoke a joint or two and turn to lead. I get a kind of routine going—wake up when I get too sweaty to sleep, boil two eggs, have a few puffs, head through the drive-thru for an apple cruller, park in the shady spot across the street, under the tree with leaves the size of my head, sit until the guy pulls in the driveway around four thirty. It's not a bad place to lay low when you owe a lot of people and one of them is your giant roommate.

This morning, the woman walked right by, so close I could hear the smooth ride of the stroller. I could hear the baby too, in the little bucket thing wedged on top, mewling like the ditch kittens out at Betty's. Nathan used to call them that because farm cats have their litters in the tall grass on the side of the highway. He used to have all kinds of weird-ass lingo for life in the sticks.

Even though there's not a cloud in the sky, birds singing their fricking hearts out, I don't even get a peek because the bucket has a domed hood. What's the point of bringing the kid out if you're going to keep him covered up like those Arab women who sit in the park, roasting in their black ghost costumes? I say let the boy feel the sun on his face.

She walked right by, looked right at me, gave a little good-morning smile. She's not young—I can tell by the skin on her knees—but not bad-looking. My madre once said that a woman's upper arms, knees and heels are sure giveaways of her age. When she was in the mood, she spent a lot of time dolling herself up and talking to me like she forgot I was a guy. "When we met, Eduardo said it was love at first sight for him because he'd never seen anyone so at home in her beauty." It sounded good, but I don't think my ma ever felt at home anywhere.

Helen. Will and Helen. Just like that, I remember the names from the form. That happens these days— just when I think the weed has fried me beyond repair, something comes to me, just like that. Helen had on big white-framed sunglasses, so I couldn't really see her face, but there was something about her that reminded me

of my grade-eight history teacher. Ms. Something—
it started with a *D*—who talked to us like we weren't
punks. She didn't even wear lipstick, but she was hot,
like maybe she used to be a beach volleyball player or
something. She took some of us under her wing, tried to
get us to go to this place called Art City, where we could
express ourselves through graffiti and pottery and stuff,
but she only lasted one year.

I can make out Helen standing in front of the half-
open blinds, talking on the phone, staring straight out at
me. I say let her.

My first day parked here, it was kind of misty, like
when the water used to leave tiny silvery beads on the
low leaves out at Keeseekoowenin. Around lunchtime,
Helen brought out the baby in the bucket, lugging it with
both hands and carrying her keys between her teeth.
It seemed to take a long time to get the thing in the back-
seat. She kept bending down and struggling with the
straps or something, her trim little ass nice and tight in
blue yoga pants, then straightening and staring up into
the drizzle. Her hair was curly like Ms. D-Something's,
and kind of damp, like she'd just worked up a good sweat
or stepped out of the shower. After a minute or two,
she finally slammed the back door and drove away.

I called Bev's cell over and over, but she wouldn't pick
up, and I had no choice but to call Ray's number. I got

the machine, and his voice made me want to drive Betty's beater straight into the mud-bottom river. "Hey, kids. We're out. Hear the beep, send us some love."

I called Faye. "I saw him."

I got nothing and wondered if she was still there.

"Olivier?"

"Yeah."

"How's he doing?"

"I didn't really see him. She carries him around in this bucket."

"It's a car seat," Faye said.

"Yeah. I think she needs a lesson on how to use it."

"Did you talk to them?"

"I'm taking my time," I said.

After about forty-five minutes, Helen came back and unloaded a bunch of groceries in mismatched cloth bags. It took a long time, since she had to carry each load into the porch so they didn't get wet. Then she disappeared inside the front door for so long that I wondered if she'd forgotten about the bucket, but then she came rushing out, tripping in her flip-flops, nearly taking a header. Still, she got the bucket out in about half the time it took to get it in.

The second day was clear, and the damp lawns smelled good enough to eat. Betty used to say that, in the morning before the dew had dried in the poplars. Nathan never got up before lunch, but sometimes I'd wake up with Betty and we'd go pick saskatoons right off the bush, and she'd sing a little, maybe Elvis or Roy Orbison, just to let the bears know we were there. Then when Nathan woke up, I'd help him make fun of her croaky voice and bad taste in music.

Just as I was cracking my hard-boiled egg on the steering wheel, Helen came out, lugging the fold-up stroller down the steps like it was going to open up any second and eat her alive. As soon as she dropped it onto the driveway, though, it opened easy as pie, smooth as a German engine. No question, someone put a lot of thought into designing the thing, unlike the beater, whose coffee-cup holder is too narrow for a large-size cup.

She got the bucket from inside, rested it on top of the stroller and started angling the thing from side to side, like she was trying to recork a bottle, talking to herself the whole time. Her black tank top showed off her thin, slightly veined arms, and for a second she looked up, as if she could feel my eyes on her, watching her struggle with such perfect German engineering. But she plowed on— as Betty used to say, "You just gotta plow, Mannie"—and then took off down the street without a glance back, her slim hips swinging just a bit, her shoulders straight and smooth above her braless back. For all I knew, the bucket could've been full of tomato-soup cans.

I lit up and inhaled like it was the last joint on earth. She wasn't my type—too bony—but not bad at all in many ways. My ma was always skinny—or *slim*, as she liked to say—and that was about the only thing you could count on. Everything else about her was like a roulette wheel—you never knew where you were going to land. When I was a kid, sometimes Ma and me would be our own party of two for days straight, eating Rocky Road from the tub until I puked on her new secondhand rug, staying up late to watch action movies until the school called and complained that I was sleeping in class. Then one morning she wouldn't get up. She would tell me I was old enough to make my own peanut-butter sandwich, that she was a terrible mother, that I was better off without her getting in the way of my development. Back then, it was the not knowing that got me. Those moods would sneak up and bite me on the ass when I least suspected it.

"Don't talk to me about mothers," Bev said one morning when I tried to tell her why Eduardo got the hell out of there when he could. "Lara is the fricking Queen of Moodyville."

I guess we had this in common, it drew us together, but sometimes I don't think she really got it, because Bev talked like she couldn't stand Lara, like she couldn't believe she, of all people, had such a stupid whiner for a mother. But me, I didn't hate my ma. I was just scared shitless of her because I knew I was like her. I could feel it—like the acorn doesn't fall far from the tree. There were times when I couldn't stop myself. I was going to explode into a million pieces if I didn't find a way to release the pressure. Then other times, it was like I was made of lead, heavy and gray and poisonous in large doses. I didn't tell Bev this, of course, because I didn't want to scare her too, or make her think I was more of a pussy than she already did. She thought she understood what it was like with my ma, but she didn't.

Betty thought she understood too, and she did in a way. She'd had some bad shit in her life. Her parents came from a band with some pretty juicy property, full of fox and elk and beaver, but the government wanted to set up a national park there and so one day waited until most of the men were out hunting and then drove in a convoy of school buses. They loaded up all the women and kids and drove them to their new home, some swampy back-water sandwiched between farms. When the men got back, they had no choice but to leave if they wanted to see their families again. But it didn't really matter anyway, because Betty was shipped off to a residential school right after that, where they cut her braids and told her that everything her parents did was stupid-ass and nasty.

Betty was the calmest person I'd ever met, but she sounded funny, like she had too much spit in her mouth and needed to hork, whenever she talked about losing her long black hair. When Nathan was nabbed vandalizing some statues of old white politicians, she stayed cool as a cucumber, told him busting things up in the dark was for pussies. When she was in the hospital, covered in blueberry bruises from the cancer, she joked that the morphine made us all better-looking, like watching those announcers on TV through a frosted lens. But when she talked about her parents, she got that spit in her voice. They died when she was young, but she said they talked to her whenever we went back to Keeseekoowenin, back to the land that was finally returned to its rightful owners. She heard them in the poplar leaves, round as coins and whispering in the slightest breeze. She heard them when the loon's call bounced off the water, high and hollow. And she heard them when the coals let out a loud, angry crack, sparks rising up orange and bright until they disappeared into the stars. She got like this after a few drinks, and Nathan would want to take off, before she got started on the legends. But it made me wish my madre was dead too, even though this made me one really shitty son.

When Helen finally came back, a brunette with fat calves was with her. She had a stroller too, a red number with three wheels and a bucket. They both unloaded their cargo, looked at me like they were checking a clock on the wall and went inside.

The third day was fricking hot. I slept through most of it because there was nothing else to do and because Warren had woken me up early with a hoof to the kidneys. He'd told me I was going to have to start earning my keep, even if that meant turning tricks behind the laundromat. I didn't care. I still had enough weed to take the edge off for another week, and the dull ache in my back wasn't all bad. At least I knew I was alive, and that I wasn't dreaming, because I was beginning to wonder if everything was a dream now.

All day, I drifted in and out of weird daydreams: Bev handing me a bundled-up blanket that turned out to be a small orange tabby, eyes still shut tight, rough pink tongue reaching for my salty thumb; Faye sitting beside me in Betty's beater, telling me Bev saw a fortune-teller when they were young who said she would marry a short dark man with quick hands. I even missed Helen and the bucket getting into the car, didn't notice until they were already back, but in my daydream, I saw a downed crow flailing on the lawn. It was choking on something and sounded so awful that I wanted to put it out of its misery. But I woke up instead, because I've always been a pussy about stuff like that, and that's when I saw them, Helen rushing up the steps, talking to the screaming bucket that sounded just like the crow. Before she closed the door, she gave me a quick look, almost too quick to notice, but I knew I was awake because it felt like someone had reached inside and thrown my kidney against the curb and then stuck it back in my body.

★ ★ ★

It's been four days now, and I think she might be starting to freak out. The sun is right in the middle of the sky, blasting through the windshield like it hates me and wants to show me who's boss. It's lunchtime and I'm hungry, but the thought of warm boiled eggs makes me want to hurl. I watch the guy pull up in his German car, watch him walk over like he wants to invite me to a barbecue. It's out of my hands now.

"You got to take life by the horns," Betty liked to say. "Don't wait for somebody to save your ass, Mannie." She made it sound so easy, like any retard could do it, but I bet Betty never felt her whole skin, every fricking inch of it, turn itchy and electric, never felt like she'd turned to lead.

He comes up to the window with his hands in his pockets. He's so tall, he has to bend almost in half. "Hey. We can't help but notice you've been here awhile. Can we help you with anything?"

Four days of waiting, and I've got nothing. Bev would tell me that to succeed in life, you need to be two steps ahead of your competition, because she's brainwashed and that's what Ray would say. Betty would tell me to pull myself together, to say my piece and be a man. But what if you're a man made out of lead?

The guy tries to look friendly and ignore the smell. The car must reek of weed, and I haven't showered in maybe five days. "There's no law against sitting," I say.

He nods, still bent in half. He's probably the same age as Eduardo but still has a full head of wavy blond hair. He looks like the guys who used to come into Ray's after work, the kind who always had a foreign beer or two and talked about sports they played, not sports they watched.

"No, there's not," he says. "It's just we're kind of curious, the neighbors too, since it's been awhile. You've been here a few days."

He laughs, still Mr. Nice Guy. I think Bev would've called him Mr. Numb-Nuts-Square-Pants or something bitchy—but then I remember she's already met him, already chosen him.

"You can't blame us, can you?" he asks.

"My kid's in there," I say.

He swats a mosquito on the back of his neck too late, and we both check out the thin streak of blood across his fingers. His blond eyebrows knit together, and the lines between his eyes get really deep. "What's that?"

"My kid is in your house," I say.

He stares at me. His back must be getting sore. "Olivier?"

"Yeah," I say.

"Are you Mannie?"

"Yeah," I say. "Emmanuel. It means 'gift from God.'"

He stands up, then bends down again. "Emmanuel, okay." He scratches his cheek, takes it away, looks at his own blood. If I were a real man, I'd say something, throw him a bone. I would save him from his misery.

"Listen," he says. "Can you stay right here? I'm going to go in and see what's the best thing to do here. Okay? Don't go. Can you wait?"

I've been here for four days—where the hell does he think I have to go? I guess he has no idea that I can hardly move, that all I can do is peel my thighs off the beat-up vinyl, one by one. I can reach in the glove compartment for the matches, light 'er up, close my eyes, sweat. Mr. Lead Man is good at waiting. He can wait for his ma to come back from the mall for hours that turn into days. He can wait for Bev to come to her senses and walk out of Ray's condo prison. He can wait for Mr. Nice to tell him if he can see his own kid. He can wait for things to come to him because there is no way he's going anywhere. I wait. I sweat. I wait and sweat some more.

Ms. De Luca, I think. That was the friendly, stressed-out history teacher.

When he comes back, I am imagining Ms. De Luca's hand on my leg. Her nails are unpolished and mannish, nothing like Bev's, and when she squeezes the meaty part of my thigh, I can't decide if I want to start crying like a baby or jump her bones.

"Emmanuel?"

I don't bother opening my eyes. "You can call me Mannie."

"We talked to the worker, Mannie. There's no visitation in the agreement. But if you want to see him, we're open to it."

I'm awake. My kidney tells me so. "When?"

"We can arrange something, but maybe not here, at the house. Maybe in the park or something."

Even with my eyes closed, I can tell he's not bent over now. His voice comes from above. "You got somewhere we can reach you at?"

I tell him my number and he writes it on a little white pad, the kind doctors use to hand out meds. "Okay then."

Time goes by, but he doesn't leave. He's breathing hard and loud, really hard and loud for a guy who looks so fit. "You okay?" he asks.

I nod. For some reason, I feel like if I look him in the eye, the heat will finally be too much and I will melt into a teeming mass of silvery sludge sliding down the burning seat, oozing over the floor mat, pooling beneath the brake and gas pedals.

"Mannie," he says, bent over again. "Can you get home?"

Will, I think. Their names are Will and Helen. "No sweat," I say.

He straightens up and stands there, breathing like a fat guy. I open my eyes, start the truck, almost run over his toes as I pull away.

★ ★ ★

All afternoon, Warren's number keeps showing up on call display, so I stay clear of the apartment. Once, he throws me off and calls from another number.

"Hey, little faggot. I can find you, you know."

I think of how Warren called Bev a slumming slut who got all her money from daddy and how Bev called him Mr. Doughboy Mobster.

I don't check my messages. I spend the night on Oak Street, not far from where I picked up Faye. It feels strange and familiar at the same time, like I'm spying on the past, on Bev as a kid, trying to find out something she hasn't told me, some clue that will help me get her back.

She never mentioned that she'd lived here when she came with me the time we lucked into a Fiat convertible on Montrose. She almost wanted to pass it up because the keys were right in the fricking ignition.

"I want to see you do it, you know, with just your hands and stuff."

"You're crazy," I said. "Get in." And she did, just before the dumb bastard inside the house made it down the front steps. We took it straight down Taylor and flew west down the Parkway until we hit gravel. The road was in rough shape, potholes with puddles the size of kiddie pools, and she started screaming like a kid on a roller coaster, arms in the air, until we ended up in the ditch. I kept going, slough water sloshing up and over the doors, until the engine died, but her arms stayed in the air, her tank top wet in all the right places. It wasn't completely dark yet, that weird blue time between day and night, and the half-built brick mansions stuck in the middle of the empty fields looked like haunted-house row on Halloween. Her cheeks were all pink and sweaty, and her shorts were so short that the softest part of her thigh bulged, delicious and smooth. Her legs made a lopsided *V* on the seat, and I suddenly felt the urge to bite into her, to taste what it's like to be so perfect.

Somewhere a dog howled, even though there wasn't any moon. She laughed like it was the funniest thing she'd ever heard and climbed on top of me. "That was amazing."

"You're amazing," I said. She laughed even more and took off her top.

After Betty died, I actually got to know this part of the city pretty well—or at least its motion detectors. But it's like those nights are someone else's memories now, someone with fast hands itching in a way that's sort of like being on speed, or that's something like sex, but not quite, not only. You get close, you scratch until it bleeds, but you never quite reach it.

I smoke and snooze, smoke and snooze. Headlights sweep over my closed eyelids, and I can hear my madre. "Aah, look at that one. I like the green and blue together— it looks so icy cool and yet it warms you right up." It's Christmastime, and she is riding high and making a cab drive us through the streets with fancy lit-up houses. I am sleepy, and she keeps pulling me against her flat chest and kissing the top of my head. It's cold enough that exhaust fog sits in the air, holding tiny ice crystals, and the colored Christmas lights float by like cartoon fireflies. "Your father's sisters clean these houses," she says. "They're hardworking girls." More kisses on the head. "I'm sorry I'm not a hardworking girl."

She has shown me pictures of her family's house in Argentina, which makes these ones on Oak Street look like shacks. Already, I know that checks come in the mail for us and that they are never enough.

"The chemicals they use to clean, they give me a rash," she says. "You know that."

I did not know that, and I want her to stop talking. I nestle in further, and for once, she gets the hint. More kisses on the head, and I'm in heaven.

When my phone rings, the sun is already up and my mouth feels like I've been sucking on dead mice. I don't recognize the number. "Mannie?"

I check out my tongue in the rearview mirror. I expect it to be covered in white fuzz or something, but nothing. Still, I would kill for a squeeze of toothpaste, just like on weekend mornings when sometimes I got up to pee, but what I really did was take care of my nasty breath. Now, I know exactly what she would say. *You think I can fricking smell you over the phone?*

"What the hell, Mannie? Are you there?"

All this time, all I've wanted to do was talk to her, but now I just want to go back to sleep, forget about the empty baggie on the seat and babies that scream like dying crows and Bev saying my name like it's something rotten she needs to spit out.

"Yeah, it's me."

"Leave them alone, Mannie."

How many times did I imagine this conversation? And still I got nothing.

"You signed papers," she says. "You have no right."

I notice there's not even enough change in the cup holder for a breakfast sandwich.

"You made me," I say. "Those papers mean shit to me. I'm the father."

She laughs. "Please. You knocked me up—that's all you did."

"It's my kid," I say. "I'm responsible."

She laughs again. "You want to be responsible, Mannie? I'll tell you how to be responsible. Leave. Them. Alone."

"It's Emmanuel," I say.

"What?"

"My name is Emmanuel."

"Jesus," she says, "it's like talking to a doorknob."

She hangs up. I remind myself that it's not really her talking—Ray is probably listening in, rubbing his fingers against her back like a kidnapper with a gun. He can't stand that she chose to have my kid, that she chose me over him, and really, I couldn't believe it myself. Sick puppies like Ray, who think they can control the universe—they'll stop at nothing.

He convinced Bev to give his own grandson away. He takes out restraining orders like they're Chinese food. He thinks he can keep her there, make her his puppet, tell her what to say, but he doesn't love her like I do. He doesn't know how tough she can be, how she presses against me after a ride, like she can't get close enough, like she wants to climb inside my skin.

I light up my last half-joint. My stomach is empty, but I'm not hungry, and I try to remember what day it is. Eight forty-four in the morning, and the streets are deserted except for the odd dog walker. It's Saturday, a hazy Saturday, a bright, white sky. I need something to drink, need to kill this dead mouse, but I'm too heavy to move. I imagine Betty walking out of one of these big-league houses on her bird legs, oversized T-shirt hanging over her round belly. She stands there, looking both ways like she might be lost, then purses her lips and sucks in the way she does when she's not impressed.

Her obit said she didn't suffer fools gladly. Nathan joked that that meant she was a bitch, but really, you could rely on Betty to tell it like it was. She was a hard-ass, but now and then she looked old and breakable, like when she wandered out into the jack pines at Keesee and knelt down with her pouch of sweetgrass to honor some dead relative, or when she stayed up watching the late movie and fell asleep in her housecoat and ratty slippers. That's the first thing I thought of when I saw Bev: hard and soft. She didn't give two shits about what anyone thought, but she was also this curvy, sexy little girl—so girlie it almost made you feel like a perv for watching her strut by in the skirt that rode up her thighs.

The phone rings again. "I'm serious, Mannie. Back off."

I have no words left.

"You can't have him. You know that, right? It's a done deal."

If it weren't for Betty, I never would've met Bev, because before Betty got sick, I was going to go up north with Nathan to learn to fight forest fires. Betty thought getting us out of the city would keep us out of trouble. "Girls love those orange jumpsuits," she said. "Go, get out of my hair and get yourselves lucky." Only that summer she needed the chemo, and I said I'd drive her to her appointments, because I figured I owed her that. My madre, she had nice things in our apartment, stuff she brought from Argentina, like jewelry and silver goblets, stuff she stole, stuff she took into the loony bin. All Betty had was a house full of sons and greasy pizza boxes and smelly used furniture, and still she let me stay. And things went pretty good as long as I was driving her back and forth in her beater, until she died and Nathan was away, getting lucky, and I didn't give a shit about anything. I made my madre's shoplifting days look like amateur hour. Then I found out Betty had left me the truck, and just like that, she started talking to me again, giving me shit in my head, and I ended up scrubbing pots at fricking Ray's.

"Please, Mannie," says Bev. "Don't be a moron. You know I'm right."

I hang up. Most summers, Betty did get us the hell out of the city. We tented at Keesee, or stayed with Betty's sisters on the rez. And now, it's a hazy Saturday in River fricking Heights, but Betty is here, looking unimpressed, and all around me are rez dogs barking at bonfire sparks, voices rising in the black night, and stars. So many stars you almost believe in Betty's jumbled-up stories about magic tricksters and the heavenly Creator.

The phone rings again, and I don't know what to do. It could be Warren or Bev calling from another line to throw me off, or it could also be Mr. Nice who stole my kid. "Mannie?"

"Yeah."

"It's Will. You got a minute?"

"Yeah."

"We spoke with our lawyer, and with Denise, the social worker. She was a little hesitant about all this but suggested maybe we could meet for half an hour or so in Assiniboine Park. The weather's supposed to be decent tomorrow. Are you available?"

Mr. Lead Man is left in the grime and wrappers on the floor of Betty's truck.

I go nuts for the next twenty-four hours, driving through the park again and again, winding around and around through the fields of picnic areas and Ultimate

Frisbee games until finally dark comes and I pass out in the zoo parking lot, where it stinks of bison shit and old popcorn oil. I sleep until families start arriving in their minivans, slamming doors and yelling at each other, then head back across the river to grab a cruller and coffee.

I park on Portage Avenue and do what my madre and I used to do when we took the bus: head across the huge arching footbridge where people eat ice cream and shoot the shit. The river is low, and the tall yellow grass on the banks has turned into a beach of nasty cracked clay. A little kid who looks like a boy in a girlie yellow hat is whacking at the clay with a stick while another toddler wobbles on fat legs, staring up at the hundreds of crazy birds who fly in giant, swirling circles, up from their muddy nests below the bridge, around this way or that, then back down to start again. One time, Betty brought us for a barbecue in the picnic area, and just as we got some good charcoals going in the fire pit, it started raining. All of us boys got stupid in the downpour, stripping down to our gitch and sliding in the mud while Betty packed everything up. By the time we got back to the bridge, it had stopped, and we ate our wieners raw on the river-bank. Betty told me what those birds were called, but I can't think of it now.

When I came here with my madre, we mostly walked through the gardens. She hated the winter, refused to wear a toque because it flattened her natural waves, and when I asked her why she chose to live in this stupid frozen place, she said, "I had my reasons." She hated winter, but she loved the goddamn flower gardens, said they reminded us that great beauty was always possible, was always around the corner, and she looked beautiful when she said it, her fingers trying to catch her black waves as they blew across her face. Most of the time I let her babble on, spewing out crap about lilies and dahlias and renewal because I liked the sound of her voice. But really, I didn't give a shit about her gardens. I wanted to go to the zoo, watch the monkeys throw food at each other, catch a freaky owl turning its head full circle.

Now and then, she actually gave in and took me to the "animal prison." One of those times, we were crossing the river and saw a guy standing on top of one of the cement walls that close in the bridge. A cop was telling him to get down. "Just grab on to my hand, bud. Come on down and we can all relax."

"I want to be alone," the guy said. "Leave me alone."

I asked my madre what the guy was doing.

"He's having a tough time," she said. "He'll be all right."

My madre had said the same thing when we saw some kid throwing a tantrum in a store. "Poor little guy," she said. "He's having a tough time."

I knew this wasn't the same thing. "Is he going to jump?"

She laughed, flicked her black hair. "That water isn't deep enough to drown in. The rivers here are like mud puddles."

I loved her then, and didn't care what was around the corner.

On the other side of the bridge, I stop at the road. The last thing I want to think about is my madre—right now, I would probably kill her for just one toke. The place is filled with hordes of dogs and joggers: big dogs, ratlike dogs, big joggers, ratlike joggers. There is some dickhead on a bike decked out like he's racing in the Tour de France, and there's a goddamn cat in a stroller. They're all going in different directions, up and down the road, in and out of river paths, and I can't seem to get my focus. I should know where the duck pond is. I used to know—I should still know. I did everything: I kept my nose clean, I delivered shitty two-for-one pizzas for my son, I took responsibility, and now I can't find the fricking duck pond.

It feels like I'm convulsing, but no one seems to notice. Then the German car passes right in front of me. Someone inside is waving at me. It's the woman, Helen, in the back-seat, beside the hooded bucket.

I follow them west maybe two hundred feet and watch him back into a spot like a hot knife cuts through butter. I sit on a bench beside the public can, trying to look casual. A woman I don't recognize, the worker maybe, is walking ahead of them and talking on her cell. It sounds like she's yelling at her kids. "There's enough for both of you. I checked. Yes, there is!"

She tucks away the phone and holds out her hand. "I'm Denise."

Something about the way she shakes makes me stand up. Bev told me a bit about Denise—how underneath her blazer are crappy tattoos. Helen pushes the stroller, like always, with the hood up. She stops beside Denise and lets down some kind of brake with her toe. A skinny chick in a hippie skirt goes by with a baby sandwiched to her chest in some kind of sling; the little foot sticking out is covered in mosquito bites. Helen takes my hand and wraps both of hers around it. She looks older close up. Will stands back, gives a wave. "We've met. Hi, Mannie."

"I'll be over there," Denise says, but we all ignore her. Helen touches my shoulder, steers me toward the stroller. She pulls back the hood, pats a yellow blanket covered in green dolphins. "He's asleep."

The head is pink and puckered and hairless, like a little old man's. There are red pimples on his cheeks, and all I can think is that I didn't know babies could get zits.

"We called him Olivier," Helen says.

My hands start to shake, so I shove them in my pockets.

"Do you want to hold him?" Will asks.

"He's asleep," I say.

"Don't worry," he says. "He's pooped. You could blow a bugle in his ear and he wouldn't wake up."

They obviously don't notice the shakes. "It's okay," I say.

Helen pushes the hood back all the way and pulls the blanket to the side. You can see tiny blue veins branching across his forehead, like he's covered in pimply tissue paper instead of skin. Only his hands look strong—little tight, wrinkly fists. They make you wonder what he's dreaming about.

Helen puts her hand on my shoulder again. I can tell she's the kind who touches a lot, for all kinds of reasons. "Thank you, Mannie. Thank you so much. I mean, look at this beautiful little person you made."

She brushes the bumpy cheek with her finger and the lips move, make a little sucking motion. Beautiful isn't the word I'd use. He looks nothing like the round babies on diaper packs, nothing like Bev.

"He gained two pounds last week," Will says. "He's a fighter, Mannie."

It's then I know I'm like those men on Betty's reserve, left with no choice but to surrender peacefully. I am backed into a corner. I am a pussy. I can't do it to these people.

The social worker brings more papers, and I sign again. I agree to a picture every birthday until he's eighteen.

That's it. I walk back over the bridge, climb into Betty's crappy truck.

Swallows, I think. They're called swallows. Betty told me it looks like they fly any which way, but they make patterns. They know exactly what they're doing.

TEN.

I go back to the apartment, walk right in, don't give two shits about Warren. I keep thinking I hear him huffing up the stairs, but no, I'm alone with three packs of instant noodles left in the back of a cupboard and some peanut butter. There's no weed to be found, but it looks like luck still has my back. When my madre finally loses it for good, Betty is there; when Warren wants my ass on a platter, he disappears. One time, I jumped off a garage roof and landed on my feet, like a cat, and Nathan told me I had a horseshoe up my ass.

I try to remember how long it's been since I've talked to him. Three months? Ten? At the funeral, he said to me, "You were there when she passed." I'd patted his shoulder, waited, thought he was maybe going to thank me.

"It should've been me," he said.

Before I can stop myself, I'm calling him up, even though the last few times he's brushed me off, seemed in a rush to get off the line. He picks up after five rings.

"How you doing, brother?" I ask.

There's a long pause. "Hey, Mannie, my man. No complaints."

I suddenly can't remember where he went to fight fires. Thompson? Gillam? "You still up there?"

A woman yells, "Is that Tommy?"

He ignores her. "Yeah, yeah. I'm living with someone. Connie."

"Yeah?" I say. "She nice?"

"Yeah, she's nice. Great legs. She's Treaty."

"Betty would be glad you're getting lucky with a nice Indian," I say.

He doesn't laugh. "She probably would've hated her."

I don't expect this. Does he mean no one was ever good enough for her boys? "Mine's Polish," I say, to change the subject. "I work at the restaurant her old man owns."

"Yeah? Nice, Mannie. Those Polish ones, they have asses on them, eh?"

"Easy, brother," I say. "You're talking about the mother of my son."

"Are you shitting me?" he asks. "No shit."

"No shit," I say.

He laughs. "Jesus, a little Mannie, man. That's scary."

"You're the one with the fricking webbed feet. Does your Treaty girl know about that?"

He laughs like he used to, like he's going to puke up a lung. "Yeah, she's kinda sick. She digs them, eh."

"You remember we used to call you Duckie? Betty, when she was in the hospice, she started calling you that again. Did I tell you that? She never said Nathan. She kept saying 'I hope Duckie is getting lucky.'"

He laughs, but it's not the same. "You never told me that."

"Yeah," I say. "She kept trying to crack me up. 'I hope Duckie is getting lucky.'"

"I didn't know," he says.

I want to make him laugh like before, but I don't know how.

"Listen. Connie needs to use the phone," he says.

"Right," I say. "Yeah."

"It's great to hear from you, man. Congrats, eh."

After that, I'm no longer Lead Man, I'm the Tin Man from Oz, who rusts up and can't move a muscle, frozen forever until someone comes to the rescue. I'm scared again, more scared than the Cowardly Lion, more scared than any pussy has ever been. And I have no idea what to do; my brain is blanker than the retarded Scarecrow's. That movie was my madre's favorite—we'd watch it over and over, even on school nights, and she'd sing that rainbow song like she had a good voice, which she didn't.

The sun is low, fallen behind the apartment block next door, by the time Betty comes back to me, pursing her lips, looking pissed. *Don't be an ass-wipe. Stop feeling sorry for yourself.*

But you don't know, I say. *You've never been to Oz.*

Don't give me that bullshit.

And suddenly my heart is fluttering like a moth at the bonfire. My whole body is fluttering, and I have to stand up, walk around, get my bearings. I turn on lights, shut them off. I open the empty fridge, close it. I start to boil, take off my T-shirt, put it back on. There is something I need to do. I need to go get Bev. I need to save her from that prick, because that's what a man does. He gets off the goddamn futon and saves his woman.

I rip the place apart looking for a pick-me-up, and the horseshoe must be rammed firmly in place, because I find a little orange bottle behind the toilet. It's covered in dust bunnies and holds three of Warren's little friends.

For the first time in my fricking life, I know exactly what I must do. Girls like Bev need excitement, they need luxury, even if they screw the staff in their daddy's dipshit franchise restaurant with free peanuts in the lounge. I knew that from the beginning; she was the whole reason I got back in the game. Girls like Bev accept nothing less than buttery leather dashboards and plenty of room to screw.

When it came to sports, I had the skills but never the stuff. Nathan was the one with the fire in his belly. "Get in there," Betty would say to me. "What are you waiting for?" But it's like I never cared enough—until I met Bev, and then I knew girls like Bev didn't just have to be saved. They had to be won.

I walk out the door, down a few blocks to the takeout Lebanese place and then it's like destiny is suddenly on my side. There's a Lexus GX, illegally parked, ripe for the picking. I can see the owner through the window, still in his business suit at 10:45 PM, chatting up the doe-eyed, head-scarved cashier who's young enough to be his daughter. It's high-risk, but I am higher, and I'm on my way before she's handed him his change.

I text Bev as I head down McPhillips, past the casino, past the Asian megamarket, heading north, north, north until I swear I'm going to run out of city. She'd said this was the perfect neighborhood for Ray, a fancy-schmancy new condo development trying to pretend it wasn't on the wrong side of the tracks.

Where R U? I've got a Lex, fully-loaded. Your fav color seats.

Ten minutes and I get nothing, but I don't worry, because luck is on my side. I've got two little friends left, dancing around in the glove compartment, and I feel ready for anything. It starts to drizzle, and the wipers come on fricking automatically. Headlights are diamonds, brakes are rubies. There's no tunes, but I drum the steering wheel like I'm at one of Betty's fricking powwows. I'm not even at the corner of Leila when she gives in.

Why would I go anywhere with u?

I don't wonder if Ray is there. Screw Ray.

Cuz u want to

I drift lanes a little and some asshole blares his horn, so I cut in front and give 'er. It's been ages since I felt so awake. The whole night is a shiny jewel. Screw Ray. She can't resist.

I'm at the condo

Asshole pulls up beside me in his minivan and flips me the bird. I give him a friendly salute, let him know I'm on a mission.

B there in 5

At the intersection, the turning light blinks green, ushering me through like a fricking beacon on the high seas. *This way, man, no stopping—tonight's your night.* The parking lot at Ray's latest shitty restaurant is none too full. The letter *B* in the sign is burnt out, so it reads "Joe lack's." The rain comes harder, and everything shines except the *B*, and then the maze of street signs begins, streetlights shining like tiny suns. I try to let my instincts guide me—I'm traveling through the stars, guided by the force. I've got to let myself go, let myself feel it, and I'll find my way.

I was there only once before, on a bright, chilly afternoon when Ray threatened to set the dogs on me before I could even talk to her, and even then the houses all looked the same, double garages with a house attached, treeless stretches of lawn, picture windows stretching two stories, blinds drawn.

I turn around, try again and again. The rain comes; the wipers have a mind of their own. This is no time to pussy out. I'm back at the main road, following it deep into the maze of streets again, no going back…when I see the condo building. Maybe five stories, set far back from the street, a U-shaped drive lined with new old-fashioned lamps. The lights are round as moons, and this is my night.

She's waiting outside, under an awning trimmed with tiny twinkling lights. The minute I see her, I know I don't feel like driving anymore. I want her to take me by the hand and invite me up. I want to give it to her in that bastard's king-size bed. I want to show her I've fricking grown up, show her what it's like to be loved by a real man.

She pulls her hood up and runs to her chariot.

"What took you so long?"

Her face looks a little puffy, like maybe she just woke up. She's wearing braids, just the way I like, but it looks like she hasn't showered in a while. I finger the messy strands of hair around her ear, need to feel that she's real.

"I missed you, babe."

She bats my hand away, playful-like. "Yeah?"

"Yeah."

She rubs the leather seat. "Nice. But this is latte, not espresso."

She's wearing a yellow tank top with spaghetti straps and jean cut-offs. She still looks a little pregnant and round. Her thigh is wet, and her nipples bask under the light of the moons.

"How you been?" I say. "You okay?"

She shrugs. "I told Ray I had cramps so I didn't have to hostess tonight."

I squeeze her thigh, have to stop myself from cutting off her circulation. There are fireworks in my fingertips, and I feel strong enough to juggle lampposts.

"Nice place," I say.

She shrugs again and her nipples dance a little jig. "He can't really afford it."

I squeeze my sympathy and she turns to face me, leans in close enough that I can see a tiny zit on her chin. Its head is white and pointy, and I imagine popping it just like that, a little spray of her pus on my ready fingers. She pokes me in the chest. "So tell me. Was it Faye?"

On a joyride, Bev always edged closer the faster we went. After a good run, hitting over a hundred and fifty maybe, she used to climb right into my lap and lick me like a cat: earlobes, chest, eyebrows. "What?"

"Did Faye tell you where they lived?"

I can't take my eyes off the zit. I want to save all of her, even the disgusting parts. I want to fly her up to his bed and let the fireworks explode in her. But she keeps talking. She keeps poking. "Hello, Mannie. Are you on something? Look me in the eye."

I look at her, hard, trying to tell her what I want without words.

She squeezes my cheeks in her hands and talks to me like I'm a retard. "Faye. Faye told you where Will and Helen lived."

Faye, I think. Why is she talking about skinny, Chinese Faye?

"Yeah," I say. "She showed me."

She releases my face and settles back into the buttery leather seat. "Of course she did."

I grip the steering wheel, hold the fireworks in a little longer. The force is with me.

"Bev. Come on, babe. Who cares? I love you."

She crosses her arms over her chest. The rain stops, and leftover drops sneak down the windshield like snakes.

"She was adopted, you know," she says.

I got nothing. I just know I need to move soon or something very bad will happen. Then she jumps up in her seat like a little girl who just got a pony. The nipples are back, waving at me, and she's patting my thigh hard to enough to sting. "You know what we should do? We should take her for a ride. You thought she was uptight, didn't you? So totally not your type. But I've seen her— she can be wild. She just needs a little encouragement."

I got nothing. Nothing but a need for release. "Bev," I say. "Please."

She moves her hand up my leg, tilts her head and begs. "Come on. We owe it to her. She took pity on your sorry ass."

Her hand moves up and the snakes slither down. I know her mind is made up, and I have to keep her in this fifty-grand hunk of metal or all is lost. Her breath is steamy against my neck. "What are you on, Mannie? That's no weed in your eyes."

I reach across her lap and she moves with me, the two of us finally in sync. The glove compartment slides open, slow and easy, at my command. We're skin to skin as she too opens wide, sticks out her tongue like my madre taking communion at mass. Her tongue is so soft and pink and wet and it's like I'm that powerful little pill sliding down, down, down. I feel strong enough to chew screwdrivers.

It's not like my Bev to need any help from little yellow friends. Thank God I'm here.

"Forget Faye," I say. "She's not interested."

But she's already moving away, already texting. "Just drive, Mannie."

She tells me to stop in front of a very big, very old, very dark house.

"Is she home?" I ask.

Bev leans back, puts her feet up on the dashboard. Her sandals look dusty, even after the rain, and I almost feel bad for the Lex. Those feet should be in my lap—I should be sucking those toes clean, and instead they're messing with perfection.

"Jesus," she says. "Patience, Mannie. You'll have plenty of time to speed things up."

She bounces her knees up and down, hugs her legs like she has to pee. Before, she never seemed interested in getting hopped up, called me Mr. Self-Medicated, called her brother Mr. Waste of Space, called Ray Mr. Functional Junkie.

She bounces. She licks her lips. She glares at me. "What are you looking at?"

"Nothing," I say, grabbing a braid and giving it a little tug. Sometimes, when I sucked her neck, she actually liked it when I yanked her hair. Hard. "Let's go, Bev. Just you and me. Like old times."

She laughs, but it's not real. "Old times? What are you, fifty?"

This is not the way I imagined it. One time in school we made volcanoes, and I still remember how it works. First the explosion, the awesome spewing of flying rocks, then the slow goo-like lava. "You know what I mean," I say.

She turns away, stares out the window. "We lived there. The one with the floodlights."

It's not quite as big as the boxy ones, but more interesting. Over the door, the roof comes to a giant point, and there's a little iron balcony on the second floor. On the front step are two black pots with little trees in them, trimmed to look like twin penises.

The lava, I think. That's the stuff that buries you alive. "Nice," I say.

The bouncing has turned to a kind of rocking. "Ray hated it. He said old houses gave him the creeps."

"So why'd he buy it?" I ask.

She clicks her tongue, turns to study the deserted house where Faye is supposed to be. "Lara, of course. She wanted to decorate a period place. She thought stuffing a place full of other people's old family pictures would give Ray the idea."

"Idea for what?" I ask.

She gives me the ol' do-I-have-to-spell-everything-out-for-you face. "Of how to be a family."

I tell myself that we can't wait forever, that there's still one more in the glove compartment, waiting to join the party. It's not too late. "My madre kept out a wedding picture of her parents even though she hated them. She said it was because her father was always a dashing bastard, but her mother never looked that beautiful again."

Bev smiles, and I bury my face in her neck, ready for that familiar smell of fruity shampoo and secondhand smoke. But then she waves and jumps out of the car.

Faye is there. Bev is steering her by the shoulders, stuffing her into the front seat. "Guest of honor," Bev says.

Faye stares at me like she's just walked into a surprise party. She's wearing the same grape-colored hoodie she had on last time, and I realize her hair is the exact opposite of Bev's: neat, straight, blue-black. Bev is already in the back, poking her head between the front seats. "Climb aboard. I warmed up the leather for you."

In the bucket seat, Faye seems to shrink even smaller. She's nothing but hoodie and knees, the total, exact opposite of Bev. "Is this Ray's car?"

Bev laughs, for real this time. "Ray wouldn't let Mannie near his toaster, never mind his Lex."

All this time, we'd managed not to mention him, which was probably some kind of fricking record. Faye stares at me, waiting, taking up maybe two-thirds of the space that Bev did.

"The jerk-off didn't even have a club on it," I say.

"It's stolen?"

Bev sticks her head right between us and dangles a braid in Faye's face. "Yes, sweetie. It's stolen. Isn't it exciting?"

This is not what I'd imagined, not where I want to be, with Bev's skinny Chinese sort-of friend in the front seat of the glorious Lex. Her parents have not sent her off to play with Bev tonight—she obviously snuck out while Mommy and Daddy were snoring. So why is she looking at me like she can't decide whether to bolt or not? Why is Bev breathing quick and hard in my ear, bringing up Ray just to piss me off, wanting something I couldn't figure out if you paid me?

All I want to do is win back my woman. All I want is for her to tell me what it takes. Why is that so hard for everyone to understand?

Bev shoves her tits into my shoulder. "Let's take her for a test drive."

She gets us in gear, and the Lex has a mind of its own. All I have to do is steer with Bev's nipples hard and happy against my shoulder. Maybe it's that simple. Who cares if skinny Faye is here? We can drive. Take her to the floor. Go just to go.

Faye does up her seat belt. "Where are we going?"

I slide through a stop sign, taste the deliciously smooth ride. Bev claps her hands, throws herself into the backseat. "The open road!"

Faye ignores her and stares at me with those narrow black eyes. "So what happened? Did you see him?"

Bev is back between us again. "Nothing happened. He took one look and chickenshitted out."

A cat darts out from behind a parked half-ton and I slam on the brakes. Bev flops forward, then back, then forward, springy as a diving board. "Jesus, Mannie!"

I watch the stupid tabby disappear behind a hedge and want to grab those little-girl braids, drag Bev from the car, kick her to the curb, keep kicking until she can't breathe and has to shut up. But she's only telling it like it is.

"They're gonna send me pictures," I say.

"Well, there you go," Bev says. "The annual picture. Now that makes it worth it, doesn't it, Faye?"

"Makes what worth it?" Faye asks.

Bev laughs again, the short, hiccup-like one she saves for telling stories about Ray and Warren. "Ratting me out. Betraying a friend. Whatever you want to call it."

The streets are glistening wet. I drive. Just drive. Go to go.

"I didn't ask to be part of any of this," Faye says. "You contacted me."

"So why are you here?"

"You said you needed to talk."

Another Ray-laugh. "So? You could've said no."

The wet streets are streaked with shiny bolts of red and white, a special effect. Faye keeps her eyes on me and I keep mine straight ahead, on my way to light speed. "You can't just cut people off like that," Faye says. "I was wondering how you're doing."

Another Ray-laugh. "No? Can't keep your eyes off the train wreck, huh?"

Faye shuts up. I fly through another stop sign and a hybrid cab wails its sickly horn. I slice by parked cars, close enough to graze side mirrors.

"You're going to hit something," Faye says into her knees, as if the crash position will do squat.

Bev powers open the sunroof and stretches out into the wet night. The air smells dank and sweet as old garbage. "You can't control everything, Faye," she shouts. "You win some, you lose some."

Then she is back dangling between us, reaching to push Faye's bony knees aside, her round hips almost nudging my ear. She opens the slick-as-shit glove compartment, empties the bottle, shoves her palm under Faye's chin. "Here. We just thought you deserved some fun. Okay?"

Puddles spray like it's the seashore. Boulevard trees fly by like we're in a Kansas tornado. Brakes squeal across

four lanes, and Bev tries to choke her sort-of friend. No—
she's trying to jam the pill into Faye's mouth.

At the Catholic boys' school, we charge through the
red like a Spanish bull.

"Cut it out," I shout.

Faye is moaning or groaning or crying. I ease up on
the gas, and Bev is tossed backward. She Ray-laughs and
rebounds, horror-movie-screams in my ear so loud that
it stings, so loud that I miss the sirens. But not the lights.

"Mannie," Bev says, suddenly stone-cold sober, all
business. "Don't chickenshit out on me now."

Faye is crying without any noise. Her hoodie-covered
fingers are gripping the door handle like she's thinking of
SWAT-rolling onto the sidewalk.

Bev, all screamed out, speaks quietly into my ear. "You
can do this. Come on. Let's do this. Let's have some fun."

Faye's eyes tell me nothing, shiny black marbles in the
shiny black night.

Bev is hot and tickly against my neck. "You know
what this means, don't you, Mannie? You're doing real
time. And I told you, I'm not cut out for the role of prison
groupie."

The flashing lights are kissing my tail now, ready to
make their move up alongside. New-money mansions
on tiny lots rise up on either side of us, like a tunnel.
Bev licks my neck.

I take her to hyperspeed, where time doesn't matter and awful daddies are left in the dust. Faye huddles in her crash ball. Bev rollercoaster-screams. We sail over curbs, peel through fresh lawns, take down trees. Bev hugs my neck from behind, holding on for dear life. We are on a fricking wild, untamed horse riding off into the night.

It's hard to breathe. It doesn't matter. It's raining diamonds.

ELEVEN

I dream of my madre. It's not Christmas morning, but she's lining up toys for me on the kitchen table. "These are not the big-box shit. These are quality."

They're all building toys, boxes filled with plastic tubes and bolts, kid-size wrenches and interlocking hunks of wood that somehow become helicopters and dump trucks and rockets. I'm six years old, and I hug her around the waist so she won't see me cry. I'm not old enough to read the instructions, have no hope of making the amazing things in the pictures. I wanted the plastic walkie-talkies I saw on TV.

She pats my head, probably thinking I don't know how she got such expensive, useless things. "You are so good with your hands for your age," she says. "Maybe you'll be surgeon. Your uncle back home—he fixes baby's hearts."

Not dreams, memories. *Baby's hearts. Stolen rockets that will never be. Uncle surgeons that I'll never see.* Stupid rhymes that make me laugh. *Ha ha ha*—a laugh with no sound.

It's the middle of the night, in June, because she pushes a math textbook off the bed. I had planned to study this time, but the apartment was too quiet—creepy quiet. She crawls in beside me and nuzzles my neck like a dog, except her nose is hot, like the rest of her. The summer heat hasn't hit, but she's running hot already, disappearing for hours on end, God knows where. "Forgive me, my little Mannie. Forgive me."

I pretend to sleep, still as a log.

"And your papa, forgive him. He was not a bad man. Just a coward. You must forgive him. Cowards can't help themselves."

I am a log. Unshakable, unmovable. Dead wood.

She starts to sing. "*Somewhere over the rainbow, bluebirds fly.*" I hug the feather pillow against my ears. It's either that or smother her with it. "It's okay, Ma," I say. "Hush now."

She starts to snore, wheezy and weak, like her singing. *Good cowards. Dead logs. Bluebirds. Hot dogs. Ha ha ha.*

It's Easter mass and madre's turn to cry. Mascara is running down her face, but she is still beautiful. The sunlight through the stained glass of groovy Jesus in a dress holding Mary's little lamb turns her skin golden. I am as tall as she is—she can whisper straight in my ear.

"Who's going to teach you to open the door for a lady? To be the man of the house? I'm not good to be a teacher, Mannie. I don't have good patience. You know that."

People beside us shuffle their feet, cough, give her a hard look. *But she does not care, she's on a tear. Ha ha ha.*

It's her birthday, which one she won't say. We're having pepperoni pizza and red wine that tastes like vinegar, but I drink it anyway. She keeps calling this the "last supper." She keeps wanting me to call her Magdeline instead of madre. She hands me an envelope like it's a present. The flowers I got her from the convenience store are stuck in an empty milk carton, because lots of things from the china cabinet are missing lately.

"Open, open," she says.

"What's this?" I ask, even though it's perfectly clear. It's a plane ticket to Argentina.

"For you," she says. "To go. It will be a surprise, for them, but they will look after you."

I want to smash the top of my wine glass against the edge of the garage-sale table, take the jagged edge that's left and slice her beautiful cheek open wide. "You want to send me there? To them?"

She looks at me, blinks her long eyelashes like I've hurt her feelings—her crazy fricking feelings. Does she not know how much I hate those people? If they'd cast her out, what made her think they'd have anything to do with me? What kind of monsters send their daughter away to face her imaginary monsters? Crazy fricking bastards, that's who.

Man of the house. Doors for the ladies. Monsters in the closet. Crazies in the bin. Ha ha ha.

Off to Betty's house I go. Mannie and I put my good hands to bad use. Ha ha ha.

"Forget me," Magdeline says.

Remember, Betty says, *don't take no shit. You have a good spirit, Mannie. Remember. Remember me.*

I can hear her. She is here, speaking to me in her no-nonsense voice.

"Mannie? Are you awake? Open your eyes, Mannie."

There are other sounds, too: whirring—a fridge maybe—creaking, another voice. "Dr. Janzen, please report to the nursing station."

"Can you open your eyes, Mannie?"

It's too bright, I say. It's pressing through my eyelids, singeing my eyeballs. "How can you stand it?"

"Stand what, Mannie? Open your eyes."

Betty is touching my arm, pulling at the hairs like a torturer. One time, she doused Nathan and me with a bucket of lake water to get us up for lunch. She will not stop until her mission is accomplished.

I open my eyes, and the searing glare lasts for maybe five seconds. The walls are light green, and the ceiling has a half-moon-shaped water stain. It's not Betty. I close my eyes again.

"Hello, Mannie," she says. "My name is Tamara. I'm your nurse. Do you know where you are?"

She is nothing like Betty. She's a redhead with gold hoop earrings. Freckles run down her neck and onto her chest, and her lipstick is glossy plum.

"A wet dream," I say.

Tamara doesn't respond. I open my eyes and she looks right back at me, as if challenging me to a duel.

"Heaven," I say. "I'm in heaven."

She's even hotter when she smiles, and I can't help doing it back, even though I hate her for not being Betty. I feel my face muscles move, each and every one, as if it's the first time they've cracked a smile.

"You're in the hospital," she says. "A doctor will be here soon."

As soon as she says it, he walks through the door, like they've rehearsed it. He's the bald, grandfatherly type, but his eyes are ice blue, like a Nazi officer in the movies. He grabs the clipboard from Tamara without even looking at her.

"Hello," he says. "I'm Dr. Dextra."

Your name sounds like some kind of fake sugar, I say. But luckily, no sound comes out.

He puts the clipboard behind his back and straightens his shoulders, standing tall for the Führer. "Do you know why you're here?"

Not amnesia, I think. I know that much.

Dr. Fake-Sugar Nazi stays standing tall, looking at me like I'm a retard. "You were in a car accident. You've broken several ribs and fractured both shoulders. You also suffered a head injury."

Just like that, I start to ache, as if having it all spelled out makes it real.

"Do you know what day it is?"

I shake my head and close my eyes to stop the tears, wish I could go back to my suffocating little memory room, where there is no sound or pain.

"Can you tell me your name?"

"Emmanuel," I say.

"When were you born?"

I'm so sorry, my little man. March is the cruelest month. The week you were born, it snowed six feet. My lips are heavy, filled with sand. The light bears down on me, strong enough to pry out secrets from prisoners. "March," I say.

"You've been in a coma for four days," he says. "Welcome back."

He doesn't sound like he gives a shit whether I'm alive or dead. I hear him move closer and bend toward me. "Do you remember what happened, Emmanuel?"

Was that four dream days or four real ones?

"Emmanuel, open your eyes, okay?" Tamara says. I picture those thin lips pumped up with glossy plum, smiling. Bev wore glossy plum too, which is why I know it's glossy plum. *Fractured shoulders. Nazi soldiers. Ha ha ha.*

"Do you remember the accident?" asks Tamara.

My right ear is buzzing. Someone was screaming in my ear. *Yes.*

"Where's Bev?" I ask.

The nurse grabs my wrist, and my dick—the only thing that doesn't ache—actually starts to stiffen. She takes my pulse, Ms. Professional.

"Bev is fine," she says.

I want them to bugger off now, to leave me and my hard-on to our pointless, painless memory dreams. But I have to know. "Where is she?"

Tamara drops my arm and takes the chart from the good doctor. "She's been released."

What does she mean, released? Do they think I fricking kidnapped her? *She wanted it*, I say to no one. *She came. It was her idea. She was the one.*

"You rest now," says Dr. Fake-Sugar Nazi. "I'll be back to chat later."

"But where is she?" I ask. "Is she with Ray?"

Tamara walks away from me. I hear her fine ass swishing in those ugly nurse pants. "We can't share patient information. You worry about yourself. Bev is fine."

Just like that, she makes it clear there's no use challenging her. Question period is over. The interrogation is done.

I am on a mission. I am flying high, moving into high gear, taking her to fricking light speed. But the evil doctor has an arsenal at his fingertips. Eyes appear, black and blank as the night, creepy quiet and full of holy judgment. Screams blow my eardrums to oblivion. Armed police come out of the woodwork, announce themselves with peeling sirens meant to break the will. Roadblocks exploding, diamonds raining, engines hissing. A cartoon trophy wife in a white see-through nightie climbing through the debris in the living room, trying to distract you with her heaving chest. A pot-bellied old guy waving his arms, swearing like a biker in his boxer shorts. Game over.

There's no getting around it—I need to escape the memory dreams, would even welcome the evil doctor. I pry open my eyes and suck in my sandbag lips. A fat nurse with a cute face and smiling cats on her uniform brings me apple juice. Swallowing is the only thing that doesn't hurt. The doctor comes and goes, like he's got bigger fish to fry. Fat Cat pokes and prods, says "sorry, sorry, sorry," but doesn't look at me. She's probably the kind who only does the missionary position and stares at the ceiling the whole time.

Tamara finally comes, her hair swept up librarian-sexy. Her uniform is light purple, and her lips are glossy plum.

"Do you feel up for visitors?" she asks.

Maybe it's Bev. I can already hear her voice. *You win some, you lose some. Let's have some fun. Was it worth it?* But I need to focus. It's a yes or no question. My scalp itches like a bugger, and if I look as bad as I feel, I'm a fricking monster. Bev and I, we'll be beauty and the beast, I think.

There's a croaking sound that is me. "Yeah."

Tamara swishes away, a deliciously round ass in square pants. The thought of Bev and Tamara standing over me in their glossy plum is almost too much to bear, but my dick is too drugged up to take notice.

Tamara comes back and I close my eyes, tell myself to fricking focus, because I have no idea who is with her. The guy is tall and skinny, with a gray beard and expensive glasses. He looks like he would've smoked a pipe back when people smoked pipes. She's butchy, with fuzzy blond hair. Her glasses are rimless, so you can see the bags under her eyes. They stand at the foot of the bed, just like the evil doctor, but they look too tired to hurt a fly. The professor seems to be holding the butch up, even though she probably outweighs him.

"We're Faye's parents," she says. "She asked us to come and see you."

I wonder if I was too quick to rule out amnesia. Or maybe it's just the drugs. Either way, I draw a blank. "Who's Faye?"

The butch looks like I've kicked her, like I've somehow offended her. "She was with you in the car."

In the car. They're talking about *what happened*, could be in cahoots with Dr. Nazi. "Chinese Faye?" I ask.

Now the professor looks like he wants to kick *me*, but it doesn't matter because he's not the type, probably hasn't hit a soul since second grade. "Yes."

I try to focus. Shiny black marbles in the shiny black night. Hoodie on the handle, ready to SWAT-roll. *It means God is with you.*

"She's adopted," the professor adds.

Of course—Bev told me that, I remember. "From China?" I ask. "You went there?"

These people don't look much more awake than me and like they'd rather be anyplace else in the world than here. "Yes," he says.

I am suddenly more awake than I've been for days, however many there's been, as if I've sucked all the energy from these strangers. All of me aches, but I don't care. "My dad's Filipino. He took off as fast as his little brown feet could take him."

They look lost, little lost sheep in expensive glasses.

"How is she?" I ask.

The mother is crying now, without any sound. Like mother, like daughter. "Her left leg is fractured in three places. There'll be soft-tissue damage from the impact, and she's covered in cuts and bruises."

It was easier for them to send me to Bev's. But they went all the way to China.

"She'll be okay?" I ask.

The mother wipes her nose on her hand. "Yes."

The father walks around to the side of the bed and crouches down. "Faye wanted us to tell you she would testify that Bev coaxed you into speeding away."

The hollow whooshing in my right ear is all that's left of the scream, the sound of fun when it gets old. "Is she with Faye?" I ask. "Is Bev here?"

The father looks up at his wife, like he's pleading for help. "No. I believe she went back to the coast with her mother."

So Bev is gone, gone, gone. Ray has lost.

The father stands up to his full height, skinny and towering like the poplars up at Keeseekoowenin. "Anyway, Faye wanted us to pass that on."

"They'll be assigning you a lawyer, Mannie," the mother says. "But what about family? Do you have anyone?"

The father squeezes my wrist, just below the iv. He should want my head on a platter, and yet he's touching my arm in a way that doesn't ache.

My old man's a coward. My madre's locked up. Betty's dead.

But I can't make my sand mouth say these words, not to these people, not now, when memory dreams all blur together and everything hurts too much as it is.

The mother has stopped crying and looks uncomfortable, like I've just farted. "No one was killed," she says. "You're very lucky."

Just as quick as I'm energized, I'm suddenly beyond tired. I can feel the nothingness licking at my earlobes, a kiss of fricking mercy—an escape from hollow, howling fun, fun, fun and these sad, strange people.

I dream not only of the past, but of things still to come, like Bev visiting me in prison. Ray has cut her off again, but her mom is with her, hovering like a wasp in August. Half of Lara is fat and the other is skinny: one thunder thigh, one stick; one flabby arm, one cut bicep. She gives me the willies, but I don't care, because Bev is there with little

Little Bear and even the sour, junkyard-dog-wish-I-were-a-real-cop jail guard has to pretend he's not getting weepy.

"I knew you'd come," I say.

Lara shuffles over on her high-heeled flip-flops. One side of her hair is dyed blond, the other red. She strokes my arm. "Ooooh. He's cute, Beverly. He looks Latin, maybe. Latin men can't be trusted, but they'll treat you like a queen."

I wish she would go away. At least my useless parents had the courtesy to bugger off. I rub my boy's smooth, fat cheek, and he laughs. "Hello," I say. "It's your daddy-o."

Bev pulls me up by the hair, embarrassed in front of Mr. Police Academy Dropout, who can't be more than thirty but has the gut of a fifty-year-old.

I overlook this. I smile, slow and sexy, pretend I've still got it in the baggy blue jumpsuit, crotch hanging almost to my knees. I nuzzle Bev's neck, pretend we're not being chaperoned by circus freaks. "I knew you couldn't do it."

"Do what?" she asks.

Little Little Bear grips my finger, strong as an ox. "Get rid of him," I say.

Lara pokes me in the chest too, but teeters to her fat side and goes down onto the concrete. "She didn't keep it for you," she says, still pointing. "That's just like a Latin man. Self-centered mama's boys. She had her reasons. Women have their reasons."

"Shut up," Bev says. "Shut up or I'll sic Ray on you."

Lara wails, "I broke my fat hip, it's broken! I tell you, it's broken" while Bev covers her ears like a little kid. "La la la, I can't hear you!"

Mr. All-I-Get-Is-This-Lousy-Pepper-Spray-in-My-Gigantic-Belt brings his belly over and scowls. The buttons of his uniform don't quite close, and I can see his belly button sticking out, just like Bev's did when she was pregnant. "That's enough. This visit is over."

I open my eyes. I'm back in the bed of pain, with its beeps and drips and mashed potatoes on a tray, its stream of nurses and doctors and lawyers who talk slow and serious with me but much more quickly with each other. *Jabber, jabber, jabber, la la la.* They tell me they're trying to lower the painkillers, to test my awareness, while the dreams keep coming, leaving me lost amid the days, amid a three-ring circus where you don't know where to look or why.

Glossy Plum swishes in and I almost shout, *It's not over, you bitch! It's never over!*

But the pain reminds me where I am. I'm where there's warm apple juice and cold peas, guys in ties hovering like flies, fat little Filipinos grinning as they change the pee bag. Plus, I know Bev would think she's nothing like Glossy Plum. She'd say Ms. Wet-Dream Nursey has a bit of an attitude, walking around like her shit doesn't stink while licking Dr. Nazi's ass. Bev would've called her Ms. Hot Snot.

Glossy Plum puts her hands on her hips and tries to look cheery even though I know she couldn't care less about my sorry ass. She and Dr. Nazi probably think I should donate myself to medical research.

"You're awake," she says, as if I don't know. "There's someone who'd like to see you. Are you up to it?"

No. Yes. It depends. "Who?"

Glossy Plum looks at her watch, which is either a knockoff or her boyfriend has a few bucks. "Your friend Faye is on her way home today."

Chinese Faye. Adopted Faye. Bev's sort-of friend Faye. She's never there in the memory dreams, not the future dreams, not the bed of pain. I have something to tell her, but what is it? *Is it stolen? So what happened? Did you see him?* I answered her questions. What could she want? What is it I have to tell her?

You can't just cut people off like that.

A giant white cast pokes through the doorway, followed by a tiny black-haired girl in a wheelchair. The left side of the small face is bruised, a giant purple hickey, and there's a red gash above the nose, crisscrossed with Frankenstein stitches. She's wearing a yellow hoodie that's so big, it looks like it's eaten her hands. Her body has shrunk even more, but her eyes are the same black.

Glossy Plum puts the wheelchair in Park and struts away like she's done her good deed for the day.

"You look terrible," Faye says.

I can't imagine what those black eyes see, and I don't want to. I focus on the gray-green swirls along the zipper of her hoodie, which look like snakes, or flower stems, or both. "You look small."

She rubs the cast with the sleeve of her hoodie, as if her leg can feel it. "Story of my life."

Twice—we've been in a car together twice. The first time, she helped me, and we got high in Betty's truck. The second time, I almost killed her. "You should hate me," I say.

She acts like she hasn't heard me. She looks at her hidden hands, and I study the flowering snakes. "I need to talk about it," she says. "I keep seeing the headlights in that giant wall of windows. It is so beautiful, but then the noise wakes me up. Crashing through a house is so loud, and then I hear her screaming and him yelling."

I'm confused. "Do you mean Bev?"

She shakes her head like I'm purposely trying to be stupid. "No. Did you know he was sleeping on the couch? We stopped inches from the guy's sleeping body, and the woman thought he was dead. But he was passed out, and she kept screaming, 'You've killed him!'"

I know what Bev would say. I almost killed some rich, drunk sugar daddy in his house of glass. But Bev is long gone, and the lawyers are circling with their fat briefcases, asking me to remember details. Chinese Faye is here with her eight-ball eyes, asking me to…what?

She goes quiet, stares at me until I have no choice but to look back. I remember what I have to tell her. "Your folks, they told me you'd testify against Bev. That she egged me on."

The staring contest goes on. "Why would you do that for me?" I ask.

She blinks, once, twice. The contest continues. "Because it's true."

She says it like it's that simple, like nothing matters more than the truth, not anything, not even love. Mr. Mass Every Sunday told me he loved my madre at first sight, but what fricking difference did it make? He bailed at the first whiff of danger.

Betty, though, she knew what had been done to her people. She knew what injustice was. But she knew what loyalty was too. She didn't turn on us, no matter what we did.

"Tell them everything," I say. "I don't care. But not that. Bev was along for the ride. Okay?"

"You want me to lie?"

"You leave that part out," I say.

"You'll go to jail," she says.

How do I make her understand? Where does she think I have to go? "I was trying to save her," I say. "That's all I was doing."

Her parents appear in the doorway, loaded down with dying flowers and *Get Well* balloons that are starting to droop. Stretch is wearing red plaid shorts and Butch's hair is a ball of fuzz. They look like the saddest-ass clowns that ever existed.

"Please," I say. "It's all I got."

She nods. "Okay."

★ ★ ★

I begin to miss my drugged-up haze—Warren would've done anything for the cocktails at Glossy Plum's party of pain. But they give me less and less and start hounding me back to life. *Time to pee, Mannie, up you get. Try putting these pegs in the holes—do your best. This is Anthony from Legal Aid. Pleas. Dates. Terms.*

They try to keep me awake during the day so I'll sleep at night, so the calendar will mean something again. Only the hounding—*do this, get the old legs moving, try that, it's important for assessment, your record ain't great, are you prepared to*—it wears me down until the need to nap drowns them out. I'm suddenly under water, and their words are garbled and far away. It's nothing like the nothingness of the pain meds. It goes in fits and starts, like I have to come up for air every few minutes, sleep without rest.

Fat Cat has just forced me to sit up in a chair, the vinyl kind that sticks to bare skin, when Faye comes again, wheeling her leg in first. Her face is less purple and her hair has been combed somehow to almost cover the gash.

For over a week, my only visitors have been Anthony, Mr. Charity-Case Lawyer, with the yellow fingernails and unibrow, and Cheryl, the chinless therapist with tests dressed up like games. "What are you doing here?" I ask Faye.

"I made them bring me," she says, as if I should know who *them* is.

I check to make sure my robe is closed, because Fat Cat barely registers as a woman and sometimes I get sloppy. This Faye, adopted Chinese Faye, she doesn't turn me on, but I don't want her to leave.

"What's your lawyer saying?" she asks. "How long?"

My head aches, as if that thin layer of skin and muscle around my ears is trying to crawl away. Once upon a time, a fine government-funded cocktail took care of such things. "Probably one to three."

"It was in the paper again. About the charges this time."

The paper. She's talking about the newspaper, and I wonder if Bev knows. She'd like that we made headlines, not like her sister's sorry death, but busting 'er up in a blaze of glory. "Who reads the newspaper anymore?" I ask.

"My mother works there," she says.

So Butchy is a reporter who cries without sound. "She the one who brought you all that stuff, the flowers and everything?"

She smiles like I've said something funny and shakes her shiny black hair. "I have a friend out east with an itchy typing finger. She heard I was in an accident and told a bunch of people we know."

"You got a lot of friends," I say.

She shrugs. "They don't know the whole story."

Yes, the whole story, extra, extra, read all about it— stolen car, smashed mansion, previous charges, reckless endangerment. *She can be wild. She just needs a little bit of encouragement.*

"Have you heard from Bev?"

Her black eyes stare. Are all Chinese so expressionless, so hard to read? "No," she says. "But so far the media is painting Bev and me as unwilling passengers."

Mission accomplished, I think. May the force be with you.

"No one else was seriously hurt," she says. "They should've been, but they weren't. Maybe you're well named, Emmanuel. One paramedic called it a miracle."

I laugh, really laugh, until the pain makes it hard to breathe. It's awhile before I can talk. "My madre believes in miracles, and she's locked up."

She looks away, like she's afraid the crazies might be catching. Then she hands me a beat-up piece of paper with something written on it: *She calls him the Little Alien.*

"Turn it over," she says. "It's Olivier's ultrasound picture."

All I see at first is a tiny black-and-white bug, but then I look closer and start to make out arms, and a head, and a backbone—maybe a foot. "She called him the Little Alien?"

She pretends she doesn't hear me. "You did the right thing," she says. "You know that, right? I'm not leaving until you know that."

But I'm already long gone. I'm in the car, on the way to Keeseekoowenin. They're shoulder to shoulder, three smelly brothers in the backseat, but I won the toss and ride up front with Betty, resting my stinky runners on a giant watermelon in the foot well. The sun is high and the sky is light, squinty blue. Like usual, there're the crazy little birds that land in the middle of the highway. They're red-winged blackbirds, even I know that, because they're all black until they take off and you see each wing tip is red as blood.

Two birds sit there for no reason until it seems the front wheels are within inches of them, and then they swoop out from under us, take off, up, up, up.

I spin around to watch them plunk themselves on the high wire of a telephone pole, and it's like they're laughing down at us all sandwiched in Betty's smelly truck. That's me, I think. A bird on a wire.

Jesus, Bev would say. *A bird on a wire? Could it get more fricking cliché?*

Faye touches my arm. Like father, like daughter. "What did you say?"

I said I don't care if it's cliché. It helps me sleep.

EPILOGUE
Faye

They don't like it, but they wait patiently for my explanation. My parents let me out of the house to visit a repeat offender, as many times as I ask—they take me there and bring me back. They swallow their disappointment, seem happy just to have me with them, back from the brink.

Celeste arrives with a new haircut, career-girl short. "So spill it," she says.

I know from my mother that Carson is history. His feelings got hurt too easily, he sulked—a muscular, well-coordinated baby. "God, Celeste," I say. "Why do you care so much?"

She pulls at her shorn locks, bangs her head against an invisible wall. "Because I thought we were friends."

It was really that simple for good ol' practical Celeste—because friends stick by each other. I'll have to introduce her to Mannie, the most loyal person I know.

"Okay," I say. "I know. I'm sorry, Celeste."

She grabs the hem of the Chinese robe, rubs it absently between her fingers as if to comfort herself. The tip of her nose and rims of her eyes are turning pink, the closest she gets to crying. At the end of sad movies, I call it *the pinkie effect*.

I hand her a pen to sign my cast. "Don't give up on me, okay?"

She snorts, shakes her head. "Your mom would hunt me down. She loves me more than she loves you."

"Shut up," I say.

So Celeste is still Celeste—and Emma is still Emma. While I'm in the hospital, Emma texts me updates. Her parents are still not speaking to Colm, but he's moving to Toronto soon. One day she's buying Kiki, another disturbingly detailed Asian doll; another, she's pre-reading her pre-med textbooks. But always, she's that dutiful, fearless Chinese daughter.

On the day my cast comes off, Sasha appears in the midst of a series of forgettable email ads for cell phones and cello camp.

To Faye...Last time I sent to you, I was very blue. My mother married a new husband and I felt like here held no promise. My country is beautiful and shitty, both at same time. Your country, Canada, not China, I would call nice. Nice. I have baby part-sister now, which is so so strange, but she is very funny. I teach her how to do the thing with the tongue you call raspberry in Canada, with food in her mouth.

I am learning art from my neighbor, who does the graphic books. I have lots of imaginings, and now I must get to work or that's all they will stay. I hope maybe I come see you again sometime. You play cello for me and I weep, because I'm so good at the blues. Sincerely, Sasha.

So Sasha is back from the brink too, no thanks to me. All those months I waited to hear from him and when he broadcast that SOS over cyberspace, I didn't even answer. All I can do now is send him a video of me playing my latest favorite, a wild, in-your-face tune by some Czech/German busker my father heard in the Toronto subway station. He bought one of the guy's CDs out of a cardboard box and added it to my playlist in the hospital.

Yesterday, I put my best headphones on Mannie and cranked it. I'm not sure he knew what to make of it, a cello going more freaky badass than any hip-hop sample, but he listened until I had to go.

When I got home, I pulled down the worn box from my closet, the one I nearly slept with for months of my childhood. I opened its fragile lid and held the tiny knit vest to my face. It smelled nothing like Sasha's sweatshirt but like a mix of old wool and harsh detergent and something else, starchy as rice.

It's yellow, with a slightly cross-eyed duck stitched on the chest. The pants are knit too, a gray-green that must've sagged horribly beneath a diaper.

"Most Chinese infant wear has a hole in the bum," my mother said. "They toilet train by just letting their kids relieve themselves in the middle of the sidewalk."

But the orphanage had humored foreign parents, supplied brand-name disposables, tried to dress us in cute outfits for meeting day. My shirt is soft white cotton with a yellow happy face in the middle, the kind that was popular in the sixties. When I was small, these clothes were my baby pictures, my one physical link to my beginnings. I searched them for clues, studied every seam, every button, but in the end, that's all there was, all they were—a collection of threads meant to keep me warm in the Chinese heat.

Now I know the clothes are a nice souvenir of a happy day, nothing more. I know the girls at the moon gate are just a lovely picture that caught my fancy during a god-awful summer vacation. I know I will never really solve my own mystery any more than I will solve the mystery of Bev Novak.

I know I have no idea, nor will I ever, if my birth mother is among the statistics of all the women in China who drink poison. Was my mother stoic or screaming as I entered the world? That woman, the one who bundled me up and left me alone in a bustling market—was she a believer, like Mannie? Does she believe that I'm okay? All I have to go on is me, and I am still young. Am I a believer?

I remember one morning during our family pilgrimage to China, I woke up early in the hotel room. It was barely dawn, but I could hear a delicate sound, like the tinkle of toasting wine glasses. I went to the window, where everything was filtered by a soft sheet of mist or smog. Down in the courtyard, maybe six floors below, there was a man. He was neither young nor old, surrounded by cages on wooden crates, and he was cooing as softly as a new father. Each time he released a latch, a dove with chimes around its ankles would take flight, tinkling its ascent through the manicured trees to the rooftops, out of sight. To this day, it's the most gorgeous thing I've ever experienced, and I can't be sure it wasn't a dream.

Because in the memory, or the dream, my father is awake, sitting up in bed, watching me.

"How can this place be so beautiful and so awful?" I asked.

He stretched his arms behind his head, revealed the ridiculous tuft of reddish hair under his armpits, already pleased with what he's about to pontificate. "Well, maybe what's most beautiful and what's most brutal are just two halves of the same whole."

It sounds like the kind of cryptic thing he might say, just to play the professor, but I can't be sure. I do know what Celeste would say about it: *You know what you need, Faye? You need to chill out. You need a massage. You need some nice heavy petting, a little tongue in the ear.*

So okay, I also know this: Some people are lost, maybe for good, but others are found.

ACKNOWLEDGMENTS

Much thanks to all those parents who have written so eloquently about adopting their daughters from China. Thanks also to Arthur Slade for his wise advice, to my editor, Sarah Harvey, for being so fantastic at her job, and to my own parents, for raising me so happy ho-hum.

BRENDA HASIUK is an award-winning short-fiction writer whose work has appeared in numerous literary journals and anthologies. Her first novel, *Where the Rocks Say Your Name*, was nominated for the Margaret Laurence Award for Fiction and the McNally Robinson Book of the Year. She lives in Winnipeg, the coldest major city on earth, with her husband, author Duncan Thornton, and loves to answer email from readers because otherwise she'd be on Kijiji, buying used stuff she doesn't need. You can reach her at bhasiuk@shaw.ca.